WARRIORS
OF THE
FIVE REALMS
PREQUEL

LULLABY
SCARS

HOLLEE MANDS

CONTENT WARNING

The Warriors of the Five Realms series is intended for readers aged 18 and above. It contains mature themes that may make some readers uncomfortable. For a full list of possible triggers, please visit www.holleemands.com/trigger-warnings

For the downtrodden—never lose faith

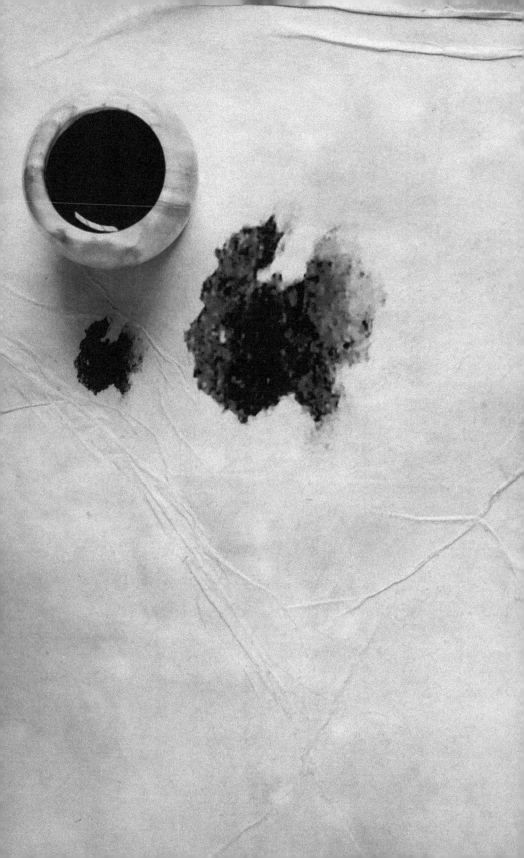

A Cautionary Tale from the Bard's Compendium

Cradled in the Southern Seas,
Lies a land of depravity,
A place where murderers roam about,
Among rapists, pedophiles, and louts,
A land where no one heeds your pleas,
The Isle of Groydon no one leaves,
A heart for you and a kidney for me,
Put a femur to broil and have some blood for tea,
From Prison Island you'll never be free.

ONE

MAILIN

Jirin, Capital of Jachuana

Most sold their souls to serve in Jirin's whorehouses.

Mailin couldn't blame them. In a land where women were worth less than chattel, and rape resulted in nothing more than an averted gaze, brothels became safe houses. Sanctuaries. If she were human, or a mage born into the impoverished caste, she might have done the same.

At the very least, whorehouses gave women access to coin in exchange for what invariably happened out on the streets. Brothels ensured a roof over their heads, warm beds, and food for their bellies. They also proscribed paupers, barring the dirty and diseased from their doors.

Unfortunately they didn't discriminate against well-paying sadists, Mailin mused at the edge of the whore's bed.

She expelled an audible breath as she surveyed the cluster of swollen bruises marring her patient's shoulder. "How could Madam

Sima let this happen?"

Leisa grimaced, angling her head to allow Mailin better access to her broken collarbone. "Madam Sima could hardly refuse a lord," she muttered through whimpering breaths.

Mailin dipped her chin Leisa's as warmth seared her cheeks, borne not of anger but shame. Of course the brute came from *her* caste. In all her years scrap-healing, Mailin had witnessed sexual violence in all its forms, meted out by men of all stations, but the jade caste lords were the worst perpetrators—misogynistic monsters hiding behind placid smiles and polished boots who derived pleasure from a woman's pain.

Monsters just like her father.

The door creaked open as Madam Sima sashayed in, the tiny baubles on her hairsticks jangling in tandem with the annoying clop of her wooden slippers. Her wraparound grenadi was a poor attempt to disguise her station. In fact, her formal attire only made a mockery of jade caste ladies. The beautifully embroidered folds of her grenadi were poorly—perhaps purposefully—slung to expose an indecent amount of flesh.

The madam tutted as she scrutinized Leisa's face. "Railea's tears, this won't do." She whirled to Mailin, hands fluttering like the wings of an agitated pigeon. "Halfbreed, whatever you do, those bruises must go. Leisa's next client is here. The man's impatient."

Mailin curled her lips but tried to keep her tone even. "The bruising is the least of my concerns. Her clavicle is broken, and I suspect there are pieces of fractured bone—"

"He's a *lord*," the madam interjected. "A foreign dignitary. We cannot keep him waiting."

Mailin folded her arms across her chest. "Have another tend to his needs. Leisa shouldn't be servicing tonight."

Madam Sima pinched the bridge of her nose and made a show of exhaling, as though Mailin were a half-wit she had to tolerate instead of a fae halfbreed for whose services she paid nothing. "He already paid. For my *best* girls."

And Leisa, for better or worse, was one of Madam Sima's best.

Mailin rose to her feet, fists curled, but Leisa tugged weakly at her sleeves.

"Maisy," Leisa murmured, using Mailin's childhood moniker. "Please, just do what you can. Powder and rouge will help conceal whatever you can't heal in time. We mustn't keep a client waiting."

Mailin only stared.

"This is why you're here, is it not? To heal?" Leisa's eyes implored her even further, saying the words she would not voice. *Help me keep my place. Help me stay off the streets.*

Mailin shook her head. "Leisa, please. If you come with me—"

"No." The firm note of finality in Leisa's tone made her choice clear. Her sister preferred life in a rookery over Mailin's plans.

She swallowed past the constriction of her throat as she held Leisa's gaze, waiting, hoping, *praying* for a change of mind. None came.

At two hundred and eighty summers, Leisa was no longer a child. She was an adult responsible for her actions, though Mailin still saw her as the young girl she'd been, barely eighty summers old on the day she was sold.

"Leisa, *please* . . ." Her sister had barely lived a fraction of her life. Mages could live to see three thousand summers. As halfbreeds born with a blend of mage and fae blood, Mailin and Leisa were equally long-lived beings. And her sister had decided to spend the rest of that life in this wretched hovel.

Leisa firmed her lips, displaying the stubborn streak they

both shared.

Mailin conceded with a heavy sigh. "All right, then." If this was Leisa's decision, then healing would be her parting gift. "I'll try my best."

By the time a maid showed Mailin the brothel's back door, Leisa was perched on some lecher's lap, her collarbone healed and her skin bruise-free.

Mailin leaned heavily against the grease-stained walls of the alley, drawing in deep gasps of air to steady her pulse. Stars clustered overhead, their glittering akin to the hushed whispers of gossiping maids as they bore witness to her discomposure. Merciful heavens, she could hardly walk due to trembling legs and strained muscles. Every act of healing drained her, and this time she had all but emptied herself for Leisa.

If things went according to plan tomorrow, Mailin would never again set foot in this place. She would never again lay eyes on her sister, who shared her blood but, sadly, not her gift.

With one hand pressed against the stone wall, Mailin inched down the alley. All she needed was to get to Ember. Her mare would get her home safely.

A gust of wind skirted by, tousling her hair and teasing the hem of her grenadi.

That was when she saw him.

A lone figure, lit by the moon's pearlescent face, stalked the far end of the alley. A soldier, judging from his stalwart frame and prowling gait. Despite the balmy night, a chill skittered down her spine. The man was so tall and broad he almost eclipsed her sight of the street beyond.

This alleyway, secluded behind one of Jirin's thriving brothels, was no place for a lone woman at night. Especially not a woman so exhausted her limbs felt like heated wax.

The man's boots clapped with confident rhythm as he

advanced. Mailin forced her spine straight, drawing up to her full height, which was meager at best.

Don't notice me. Please keep walking . . .

His steps slowed to a pause.

"Do you require assistance, madam?" His voice, low and gravelly, held a southerner's clipped cadence. The voice of a cold-blooded killer if she'd ever heard one.

Mailin shook her head, not trusting herself to speak. She could attempt to push past him, but from the look of his long, well-thewed arms, she doubted she'd get far. Her only other option was to return to the brothel. After all the whores she'd healed for free, surely Madam Sima would afford her shelter?

Decided, she scuttled back, but her legs wobbled. Mailin caught herself by digging her nails into the wall's pockmarked surface.

"Madam?" The man's voice softened, which somehow made him even scarier. To her dismay, he stepped closer. So close she scented a combination of leather and horseflesh with something deeper, muskier, and not all that objectionable.

She drew in a breath to solidify her spine. "Kindly leave me alone, sir."

He didn't move.

Mailin risked a peek at his face, and her breath stalled in her throat.

He loomed over her, a formidable figure with alarmingly masculine features. His hair was tied back, baring a widow's peak that accentuated the hard-hewn lines of a bearded face. His strong nose might have once been straight but was now slightly crooked. A brawler. The lines lacerating the swarthy bronze of his cheek were testament to that fact. His scar was not some rugged souvenir soldiers sometimes wore with battle-won pride but a brow-raisingly stark monument to terror. Thick, white, and ropy, it bisected one brow—as though a dagger had scraped past his eye and carved down to his cheek—before it forked like a snake's tongue to disappear into his beard. *Hideous.*

Mailin swallowed hard.

Logic told her he had to be human, for mages rarely scarred, and even if they did, they never scarred so badly. Yet her senses told her otherwise. An undercurrent of power radiated from this man like a dense cloud of mist shrouding a waterfall.

A mage. No question about it.

"Are you hurt?" he asked with a frown.

Never had she seen anyone more menacing, yet . . . she couldn't look away. Despite the hardness of his features, an unexpected kindness pervaded his eyes. Dark eyes that drew a woman's gaze as surely as the moon did the rising tide.

Mailin blinked, trying to break the hypnotic spell of his eyes, only to see his pupils dilate as they focused. He was staring down at her as though he'd found a rare jewel among a river of stones.

She grew unreasonably warm, the wraps of her koshiyin suddenly too tight. She shifted back until her calves scraped the wall. Like a predator sensing its prey about to bolt, he moved to trap her between his arms.

"What are you doing?" Mailin demanded, but to her dismay, her words came out hitched. Regardless of his off-putting scar, there was an undeniable savage beauty about him. A wildness contained within the civil facade of this man kept her paralyzed like a deer staring into the face of a lion.

She was so focused on the hard lines of his face that she didn't realize he'd moved again until his callused fingers skimmed the edge of her jaw, igniting heat over her skin.

Perhaps he was telepathic and somehow controlling her mind. Stealing her sanity. Or perhaps he was telekinetic because she stayed still, her feet rooted to the ground, while he caressed her cheek as though he'd every right.

"Beautiful." The word rumbled from his throat, the roughness of his timbre stroking her senses like sun-warmed sand against sore muscles.

Mailin's lips parted to draw in some air because she couldn't breathe any other way. His predatory gaze, the egregious scar, and the muscles cording his forearms formed an intoxicating blend that compelled her to do crazy, impulsive things. To reach out and touch him like he was touching her. To feel the beard on his jaw graze her skin . . .

"How much?" he whispered, tracing a finger over her cupid's bow. He rubbed her lower lip back and forth until her breath hitched. She drew in another breath before she fully grasped his words.

She blinked. "What did you say?"

He ceased toying with her lips, and dipped his head lower so his mouth hovered a bare inch from her ear. "Your price, temptress."

Her eyes widened, his spell broken. She shoved against the breadth of his chest, but the man did not budge. He merely frowned.

"Whatever your price, I assure you I will pay it." His lips grazed her earlobe, the warmth of his breath a delicious current of sensation spreading over her skin.

"Unhand me," she snapped, her senses returning like a bolt of lightning streaming into the earth. That was when she noticed his attire. The plain black tunic and leather trousers. The lack of a gentleman's surcoat. The metal ring around his neck—a collar. A *bondsman*? One who thought her a whore.

She pinned him with a glare.

Amusement flashed in his eyes, a slow smirk curving his lips, which only added a rakish allure to his features. "I'm not the one with my hands full." His biceps rippled, making a show of where his hands were—firmly planted on the wall at either side of her head.

Mailin withdrew her own hands, which had somehow latched to the tunic on his chest. Somewhere along the way, she had clung to him instead of the damned wall. Heat suffused her cheeks. Insanity! What had the devil done to her?

She tightened her lips, disgusted with herself. "Could you move? I must be going."

Obvious reluctance replaced the amusement in his eyes. A large hand clamped over her wrist, the strength in his grip reminding her that he might not be a sadistic lord, but he was still capable of violence. His scar told her he'd faced brutality, and his domineering stance warned her he had likely dealt his own.

"Wait," he said. "I can pay you. I need—"

"Take your needs to the brothel," she said with a snarl. "I'm no whore."

His fingers loosened, but he did not release her. Mailin did not wait for him to reconsider. She rammed an elbow into his hard abdomen and grimaced. It was like slamming into a brick wall. Ignoring her throbbing joint, she brought up her knee.

He had clearly anticipated the move, for he sprang back, scarcely avoiding what would have been a well-aimed blow to his prime jewels.

His lips sealed into a seam, and his eyes narrowed.

Mailin's heart thudded at the sight—not from fear but an insane and inexplicable desire. Annoyance had never looked more . . . alluring.

"If not a whore, then what are you doing around these parts, *madam*?" he asked, sarcasm oozing from every syllable.

Mailin scrambled down the alley, drawing as much distance between them as possible before releasing a long, shrill whistle. To her relief, distant hooves thundered in response.

She threw a final look over her shoulder, wrestling with the irrational part of her that wanted to go back and ask his name. A bondsman who had no place in her life. A man she would never see again should tomorrow go according to plan—and she would damn well ensure it did.

"That's none of your business, kind *sir.*"

She turned and fled.

TWO

KILLIAN

The devil take him.

Still rooted in the alley, Killian scrubbed a hand down his face and blew out a shuddering breath, trying to cool his heated blood and hardened flesh. What in the five hells had just happened? He had never wanted a woman so badly, so desperately he'd be willing to do anything. To pay *anything* for one glorious moment with her.

Madness! What had he been thinking? But Railea, goddess of light, the moment he caught sight of her face . . . he hadn't been thinking at all.

He squeezed his eyes shut.

He couldn't remember the last time he'd lost his wits at the sight of a woman. Then again, he'd never encountered a woman quite so . . . perfect? He frowned. No. Her jaw had been too square to fit the molds of conventional beauty, her eyes a little too narrow, and her lips a touch too wide. Yet her features worked in perfect synchrony to stir his blood.

Everything about her demanded his attention, from the glossiness of her pin-straight hair to the warm sandalwood hue of her flawless skin to her arresting gaze. She had stared right back at him, unflinching and bold, as though she saw past his scarred skin and truly saw *him.*

Killian had never been one to hike up a woman's skirts in a dark alleyway. A self-demeaning laugh escaped his throat. He'd never hiked up a woman's skirts in his life, but he'd been aroused enough to take her right here against the wall had she consented. He shut his eyes and pressed his forehead to the stone. *Blazing hellfires.*

He was in no position to lust after a woman, especially one who wasn't even a pleasure worker.

Of course she wasn't. Grim satisfaction filled him.

A woman that fine couldn't possibly belong to a place so wretched. He had noticed, quite belatedly, her wraparound dress that was unique to the upper classes of Jachuana. Then again, perhaps he was mistaken. What would a lady be doing in these parts of Jirin? Either way, it was a wonder she had allowed him close enough to touch.

Shame welled in his throat to replace the satisfaction.

Of course she had.

He had all but pinned her to the wall like some randy mongrel. His lips twitched as he recalled how close she'd come to emasculating him with her knee. The little temptress might resemble a delicate, sculpted doll, but she certainly was not made of porcelain. A pang struck his chest when he realized he hadn't even asked for her name.

A bitter laugh escaped his throat.

And what, precisely, would he have done with the knowledge?

He wasn't made for one as fine as the little temptress. No, he was better off forgetting her altogether, but the pang twisted deeper as he replayed the silken softness of her skin under his touch. What he wouldn't give to see her again . . .

He drew in deep breaths and allowed himself a few more moments before he forced all thoughts of the encounter from his mind. With his composure restored, he marched through the brothel's door into the cloying scent of perfume laced with sweat and sex.

A lurid painting of nude, nubile bodies wrapped in tantalizing positions dominated the room, whetting the appetite of eager patrons and souring his own. He turned toward a bevy of women wrapped in skimpy silks and seductive satins.

They glanced up at him with inviting smiles, until they caught sight of his face. If his scars didn't scare them, his collar would. They shrank back, as they always did. No woman ever saw beyond his appearance. None—until the little temptress, who had stared right back at him in return. Not in fear, but . . . fascination.

A woman with birdlike features and an ample bosom fluttered up to him. "Madam Sima at your service, good sir. What can I . . ." Her eyes widened at the scars on his face. Her smile flattened further at the sight of the silver band encircling his neck. "My girls don't come cheap," she said in a dour tone.

Killian stiffened but swallowed his pride. "I'm here for Lord Teranos."

She raked him with her gaze and gave an indeterminate sniff as though she couldn't be sure he had spoken the truth. "The *high mage,* Vale Teranos?"

Killian nodded.

Another wrinkle of her nose. "Yes, well, His Lordship has already begun making himself . . . comfortable. Can't this wait until the morning?"

For a moment Killian debated the wisdom of the madam's suggestion. What he'd learned wouldn't alter tomorrow's outcome—Vale was already set on his choice. Yet years of conditioned servitude had him saying, "He is expecting me. Take me to him."

With obvious reluctance, the madam led him up a narrow staircase to the second floor, a dim and dingy corridor lit by an occasional oil lamp. The well-trodden carpet and timeworn walls reeked of desperation. Flickering shadows danced to the muffled moans from behind closed doors.

Only at the very last room did the madam halt and knock. "Lord Teranos?" Madam Sima called, raising her voice to be heard through the hardwood door. "I hate to impose, but your bondsman is here."

A lengthy moment passed before the door opened. Pungent smoke wafted out before a woman clad in nothing but a vacant smile. Killian's ears heated as his gaze landed on the secret places of a female that were usually hidden from his sight.

"If you're lucky, perhaps your master will deign to share," the madam whispered with a sly simper. More warmth crept down his neck.

Killian kept his sights on the threadbare carpet as he strode into the room.

Vale reclined on a divan, legs outstretched, hands toying with a leather crop like an emperor in a palace of promiscuity. Another naked woman knelt between his legs, her head bent, her bottom already covered with welts.

"Lord Teranos," Madam Sima cooed. "I'm terribly sorry for the interruption, milord, but—"

"Scar! There you are!" Vale interjected with a wide grin that meant he was well and truly soused. The woman who had opened the door for them sashayed to the edge of the divan and reached for a wooden pipe, the source of the stench in the room.

Killian drew his lips into a flat line. Judging from Vale's

abnormally dilated pupils, the high mage had once again overindulged in the worst kind of substance one could inhale through the end of a pipe. Rexweed brought out the worst in men, and in Vale it often manifested in the form of violence.

"Vale . . . ," Killian began.

"Oh, five burning hells, spare me," Vale drawled with a roll of his eyes. The woman brought the pipe to his lips, and Vale took a heavy drag with his gaze locked on Killian's as though daring him to intervene. When Killian kept his silence, Vale blew out a puff of smoke through a satisfied smile before he patted the head of the woman between his legs. "Faster, little dove."

His gaze wandered back to Killian. "Now tell me . . . where've you been, hmm?"

Killian suppressed a sigh. "I could not locate a proper stable, but I found an innkeeper willing to take our horses for the night."

"Ah . . . the horses. Yes. Yes. Ah, yeess!" Vale let out a long moan, basking in the moment with his audience while the whore between his feet made a faint gagging sound. Killian shifted uncomfortably and stared at the wall's wainscoting, wishing he had chosen to risk the high mage's ire instead.

"Where were we?" Vale opened his eyes and released a contented chuckle. "Ah, yes, the horses. Took you the whole evening to settle two damned horses?"

Killian ignored Vale's jibe in favor of relaying what he'd garnered thus far. "I spoke to some of the locals. None were eager to speak of the girl. But I gathered enough to know all was not what it seemed in the correspondence you shared with Lord An Jin. There is very little known about his daughter. It's almost as though she's been raised in isolation."

Vale rolled his eyes again and took another drag. "So?"

Before Killian could respond, the madam, who had busied herself with the collection of empty ale bottles, cleared her throat.

"You're referring to Lord An Jin and his halfbreed daughter?"

Killian fixed his stare on the whoremistress with renewed interest. "You know of them?"

Consternation twisted the woman's features. "Well . . ."

The whore between Vale's legs lifted her head. "Madam Sima . . . ," she managed in a rasping voice, her words almost a warning, before Vale shoved her head back down.

"Did I pay for you to speak, girl?"

Madam Sima emitted a nervous laugh and wrung her hands. "Forgive Leisa, milord. Yes, I know of them, but it simply isn't my place . . ."

Vale pulled a pouch from the pocket of his surcoat and flung it toward the whoremistress. It landed with a heavy thud, and jaroobis spilled out at the madam's wooden clogs. "You will tell Scar all you know of the An Jin household."

Madam Sima dropped to her knees and pinched up the copper pieces like a crow picking at a cadaver's bones. "Of course, milord. Of course."

While the madam rattled off facts about the An Jin family that Killian had already gleaned on his own, overt tension radiated from the still-kneeling whore. She exuded the same undercurrent of resistance he'd encountered thus far whenever he queried about the jade caste lord.

When the madam's information dried up, Vale dismissed her. She retreated with the jingling pouch clutched to her breast while Killian made his way to the divan.

"Scar," Vale crowed, waving the leather crop in his hand. "Glad you're joining us."

Killian gave a curt nod.

It was no secret the high mage enjoyed spectators, especially when his blood was pumped full of liquor and his lungs coated with rexweed. That was when he was most likely to leave the women roughed up. Killian made a poor voyeur, but that had never discouraged Vale. In fact, his resistance only made the lord more zealous in his attempts to goad him where women were concerned. Killian had long since learned it was best he stayed.

Vale wrapped an arm around the woman beside him and hauled her onto his lap, though he directed his next words to his bondsman. "Sit."

Killian sat.

"Now . . ." Vale fondled the whore while he cocked his brows in a taunt. "Tell me, which would you prefer?"

Distaste rose bitter at the back of Killian's throat. He reached for the pipe and took a drag, then blew out the smoke. Railea, how he loathed rexweed. "You know I prefer watching."

Vale laughed, clearly having expected his response. "Suit yourself."

As the high mage turned back to the women, Killian reached into his tunic pocket to pull out a packet of finely ground powder. He tipped in the usual dosage and took a few experimental puffs. The effect was instantaneous—his muscles uncoiled, and the world seemed to tilt. Perfect.

One of the whores reached for him to slide her hands under his tunic. He shrugged her off—he wasn't that inebriated yet—and shoved the pipe into her hands. "Lord Vale needs more of this," he said, struggling to keep the slur from his voice.

Obediently, the whore pressed the pipe to Vale's lips.

The high mage was already intoxicated. A single heavy drag was all it took for his body to go limp and his eyes to close. The whores stared at their patron in dismay.

"Wh . . . what happened? Why won't he wake?" asked the one called Leisa as she patted Vale's cheek frantically, panic in her tone.

Killian chuckled as the women shook the senseless high

mage by his collar. "Worry not." He scooted over to reach into Vale's surcoat and search for the pouch. "He'll wake in the morn."

He always did. Then there would be hell to pay. Hopefully Killian had calculated the dose correctly this time, and Vale would wake with enough of a headache to forget the night.

Killian fished out some coins and dropped them into the women's hands. From the blank stares they gave him, they'd likely never received direct payment from patrons.

"Help me move him to the bed."

When Vale was tucked beneath the covers, the women turned to him warily. One said, "Where would you like us . . . milord?"

Killian meant to scoff, but the rexweed in his system wrung out a chuckle instead. "I am as much a lord as you are a lady." He made his way back to the divan and helped himself to the bottle of ale on the side table. "Consider yourselves done for the night."

They didn't need to be told twice. The women collected their clothes and scurried out the door before Killian had taken two swills from the bottle. He sighed and stretched out his legs, but the divan was too small, so his legs dangled off the armrest.

Staying had been worth it. At least he had saved two more women from a beating tonight.

A soft snore came from the bed as Vale thrashed beneath the covers, fitful as always.

Killian drained the bottle, waiting for drowsiness to catch up to him. The temptress's beguiling gaze flitted across his mind's eye before he firmly shoved her from his head. He turned his thoughts to the next day instead. Vale must be more nervous than he'd let on if he'd resorted to rexweed tonight.

Nervousness meant anticipation, and that was a good thing. Perhaps this woman—a bride Vale had been intrigued enough to travel all the way here to collect—would be the one to tame the high mage's vices. Killian shifted on the tiny divan, pillowing his head on his forearm as the effects of rexweed dragged his lids shut.

He hoped Lord An Jin's mysterious daughter was a woman of fortitude. Anything less and she likely wouldn't last her first night with her intended. At least, not with her soul intact.

THREE

MAILIN

Today was the day.

Mailin meticulously applied kohl to her eyes, rounding the edges to give herself a more doe-like expression. Men liked that. They appreciated innocence in a woman the same way wolves appreciated rabbits and deer. Leisa had taught her that while men sought sensuality in a lover, they preferred purity in their wives.

To wring a marriage proposal out of one, Mailin would have to exude both.

Satisfied with her appearance, Mailin parted the doors of her wardrobe and set her hands on her hips. The long folds of her grenadis greeted her in a shimmering array of the lightest pink to periwinkle to the deepest plum. She took her time grazing each one with her fingertips, caressing them as reverently as another woman might the most precious of jewels.

Mamma had been a seamstress who adored vivid fabrics, fripperies, and finery. Jiiyi An Jin might have married a lord, but she never did stop sewing her own clothes—and now they all belonged to Mailin.

She paused on a garment, one of Mamma's favorites. The koshiyin—the inner piece—was a swath of cerulean cotton meant to wrap around her bust and waist. The grenadi, worn over the top, was a length of azure silk adorned with swallows and hemmed with silver. She took her time dressing, layering the rich folds with care so they hung gracefully over her shoulders. She completed her attire with a matching velvet band wrapped over her middle like a wide, high-waisted garter belt.

Her fingers trailed the edge of her sleeves, rooting for the little secret her mamma had left on the inner hem of every garment. A smile slid across her face as she found the tiny embroidery of a purple bear and a jumping black rabbit. Mailin began to hum, twirling the folds of her grenadi to the tune of her favorite lullaby.

Twirl, twirl, little squirrel, swirl around like a dancing bear . . .
Shy, shy little rabbit, skirting every clever snare . . .

Lyrics Mamma had sung often. Today, Mailin would be the rabbit. Today, she would finally fulfill Jiiyi's dying wish and live the dream her mamma had always wanted. And she would do it wearing her mother's favorite dress.

"Do I look good enough to tempt a man into wanting more, Mamma?" she murmured as she studied her reflection. The woman in the mirror barely smiled, her lips painted, her cheeks rouged. She couldn't help but think she looked a little too much like the women who worked at Madam Sima's.

Mailin's fingers rose absently to her lower lip, remembering a stranger's callused hand and gentle touch. *Beautiful*, he had called her. Would he think her beautiful now?

Frowning, Mailin jerked her hand away.

He had no business invading her thoughts, especially not on

the day all her plotting and scheming came to fruition. Today, only one man's opinions mattered.

Lord Vale Teranos. A high mage well known for his collection of horses, women, and his vast lands filled with maize. The latter made him her target. It mattered not to her that he was a rake, only that he was a lord whose wealth stemmed from cropland. It didn't even matter what he looked like, but she prayed *he* liked what he saw.

If he did and made a proposal, her father would have no choice but to accept. No one, not even the lofty Lord An Jin, could afford to deny a high mage's proposition. Especially since that high mage came from a province whose archmage had recently defeated Jachuana's own in a deadly conflict of flame and frost.

Mailin exited her room with her head held high even though no one loitered around. Apart from Cook, there were no other servants left in An Jin manor, not since Mamma's death. She went down the stairs, her slippered feet soft on the steps, and paused by the dining parlor's antechamber.

She drew in a deep, steadying breath. Her father's presence always reduced her to the little girl who had once hidden in her mamma's wardrobe and peeked through the slats when she was not supposed to.

Mailin exhaled. She was not that girl anymore.

Seated at the head of the table, Lord An Jin was too busy spooning his morning meal into his thin-lipped mouth to notice her presence. He wore a customary stiff, black surcoat, his sleek, black hair hidden under a jade- and ivory-studded headpiece.

"Father." Mailin lowered her head in a customary bow.

Cutlery clinked against porcelain. The shrewd eyes Mailin had always likened to hard coals narrowed as he took in her appearance.

"Why are you dressed like a harlot?" He had never approved

of Mailin wearing cosmetics or her mamma's dresses. His dislike only provoked her to wear them.

Mailin raised her brows, feigning nonchalant surprise as she glided to the long table to take her place at the furthest end. "Have you not read the missive?"

"What missive?"

"The one I left on your desk weeks ago. A high mage from Amereen is calling today." Mailin smiled as she helped herself to a small bowl of steaming broth Cook must have left for their breakfast. "I assumed you knew."

"What are you talking about?"

"Lord Teranos is calling today," she repeated calmly.

Her father's brows slashed up. "Teranos? *Vale* Teranos? The blackguard who owns half the towns and farming villages along the southeastern border?"

Mailin pulled a still-warm bread roll from a dainty basket. "The very same."

Lord An Jin blinked, his whitening knuckles the only show of the alarm that must be growing in his chest. "And why would a high mage from Amereen be calling on *us*?"

She only smiled by way of response.

Her father sputtered, half rising in his seat as a delightful shade of puce darkened his complexion. "Devil child! What have you done?"

Mailin took a delicate bite of the bread dipped in broth, forcing herself to swallow as she carefully evaded her father's question. "I am three hundred and twenty. More than marriageable."

"Marriage?" Father scowled. "Is that what you yearn for, you shallow-minded chit?" He issued a scornful laugh. "After what became of your mother, I thought you'd know better than to entertain such fanciful notions."

Mailin tightened her fingers. Her father knew exactly where

to aim his words to best draw blood, but she kept her hand steady as she brought the teacup to her lips. She would not give him the satisfaction of seeing how much it pained her to hear his black tongue speak of her mamma.

"Besides," he added with a snort, "a marriage would require a dowry . . . Why would I pay one when the Keep would pay gold bullions for you?"

The food in her mouth soured at the mention of the Keep, the academy where women trained to serve the Echelon of Archmages—in every imaginable way. Glorified whores.

Mailin took a small sip and set the floral teacup back on the saucer, keeping her gaze serene and her smile sharp. "I thought you were more ambitious than that, Father. You'll only get paid if I'm chosen by one of the Echelon. Even then, there are no guarantees an archmage will claim me. Surely you've heard of the hundreds upon hundreds of ayaris languishing at the Keep unclaimed."

A disparaging smile lifted his lips. "Our Lord Archmage Chikere goes through multiple ayaris every year."

Mailin cringed inwardly, but she forced an indifferent shrug. "That may be so, but the Keep trains hundreds upon hundreds of ayaris each decade, all for the use of eight archmages. They are spoiled for choice, and there is nothing remarkable about me."

"There is certainly nothing remarkable about your appearance," Father agreed with a contemptuous snort. "No matter how you try, you'll always be a poor imitation of your mother. A goose trying to impersonate a swan." Father reclined. His cruel sneer scored furrows in her heart no matter how she tried to remain unaffected.

"No matter. You're bound to be claimed." He puffed out his chest, and for a moment Mailin could almost mistake it as pride in her, but she knew otherwise. Had she been a son, perhaps her father would have truly been proud.

Unfortunately, Jiiyi An Jin had borne him only daughters.

"Any archmage would relish the chance of siring halfbreed heirs. The blood running in your veins alone makes you a novelty."

Mailin unfolded a napkin and daubed the edge to the side of her lips with dainty precision. "So I may be, but you stand to gain nothing by sending me to the Keep. At least not for another ten turns of the sun."

Ayaris trained for a full decade before they were paraded before the Echelon to be selected.

Mailin drank another sip of tea, allowing her words to sink in before adding, "However, if you allow Lord Teranos to take my hand in marriage, you will immediately secure an alliance with one of the most influential men in Amereen." She met her father's flat eyes with a smirk. "At no expense to you. He has agreed to forfeit my dowry should he find me a suitable bride. In fact, should today go well, he would go as far as to pay ten thousand jaroobis for my hand in marriage."

For the next instant, there was nothing but shocked silence and her father's breathing. Mailin took a bite of the soft roll, forcing herself to swallow even though apprehension turned the bread in her throat to stone.

"The blackguard offered ten thousand jaroobis for you?" He spoke as though he had never imagined her fit to be anything more than an ayari.

She gave a curt nod. Before her father could come to the notion of possibly selling her to another high lord of his choosing—the very reason she had chosen to inform him of Lord Teranos's arrival at the last minute—Mailin quickly added, "You know I would never go against your will, Father, should you insist I go to the Keep. But I do imagine Lord Teranos would be rather disappointed should you decline. After all, he will have traveled at least four grueling days through the Southern Seas, maybe longer if he came by horseback . . . I wonder what a man of such import would do in the face of disappointment?"

Mailin settled the napkin back in her lap and donned a silken smile. "I suppose it depends on whether he holds the ear of the lord archmage Thorne."

At the mere mention of the neighboring archmage, a visible shudder spilled down her father's frame.

"You wretched creature." Judging from his darkening countenance and trembling fists, her father had finally realized how she'd managed to set it all up without his knowledge. "You forged my penmanship? Stole my seal?"

Mailin sipped the last of her tea and pushed away from the table. "It was just a letter, Father. Lord Vale Teranos is young and unmated. I saw an opportunity for the both of us and acted upon it. You've always wished to trade me for coin, haven't you? I merely saved you the trouble of doing it yourself."

"Ten thousand jaroobis." Father scoffed. "You've overestimated your own worth, girl. I won't be surprised if he takes one look at you and decides this was all a waste of his time."

Mailin straightened the folds of her grenadi, metaphorically shaking off her father's words. "I'll be sure to remind him of the *novelty* of my bloodline." She smirked. "Even a plain goose can be a prize if it is liable to lay golden eggs."

She turned on her heel.

"*Twenty* thousand." His words seized her steps.

Her father steepled his fingers. "Twenty thousand jaroobis, and it'll be worth my while to play along in your wretched schemes." A shrewd smirk stretched his thin lips. "An ursi less and I'll take my chances, even if it means offending a high mage. I may never receive a single gold bullion in return, but I'd rather see you rot in the Keep."

FOUR

MAILIN

Mailin's heart hammered in time with the pounding of the hooves on her driveway. She peeked between the drapes of the parlor windows, and her heart rate ratcheted even more. Two men on horseback cantered up the driveway.

She frowned. Only *two* riders? She had expected a high mage to travel with a full retinue.

She smoothed out her skirts, hurried to open the front door, and froze. In plain daylight, his scar stood stark against the bronze of his skin, his collar a cold and unyielding band of silver glinting at his neck.

Mailin blinked.

He stared right back at her, his shock mirroring her own. Then he proved himself real by saying, "*You* . . . What are you doing here?"

Goddess of mercy, the rough bass of his voice was even deeper than she remembered, filling her ears like low thunder in a summer storm.

"Me?" She tried not to sputter. "Who are *you*?"

"Do not let his ill manners scare you, my lady," interrupted another masculine voice from behind the bondsman. Polished leather boots strode into view, attached to long legs clad in fitted leathers and a lean body. "Scar may appear scary, but be assured, he will cause you no harm."

Mailin stared at the stranger, focusing on the sigil of the Amereenian court embroidered on the mandarin collar of his shirt. A golden dragon. Unlike the bondsman, this man's dark hair was cropped short in the manner of Amereenian noblemen, his face clean-shaven. He smiled wide, revealing a row of perfectly white teeth.

"I'm Vale Teranos, the high mage of Amereen."

The man who had the power to free her from under her father's thumb was finally here.

Once they'd completed a formal welcome, where her father had stiffly, albeit politely, exchanged pleasantries with the high mage, Mailin led Vale to the tiny gazebo atop a grassy knoll on the manor grounds. She tightened her fingers over the gazebo's handrail, fighting the urge to turn back, confront the bondsman, and demand more answers. Had he known who she was all along? Yet his shock at seeing her had seemed genuine. She shot Vale a small smile before throwing a discreet look over her shoulder. Scar remained a solitary figure leaning against the manor's russet brick walls, ostensibly keeping a distance to allow her and Vale privacy for their conversation.

Scar. Surely that couldn't be his real name? Her head spun. The man who had inspired her illicit thoughts served the man she sought to con. The gods must be having a laugh at her expense.

A chuckle sounded in her ear, startling her back to reality. "Most impressive," Vale said as he surveyed her family's estate. "Does this all belong to your family?"

Focus, Mailin!

Mailin shoved all thoughts of Scar from her mind and conjured a bright smile. "Yes, my lord. My family supplies Jirin with most of its barley."

She had chosen this location for her first conversation with Vale for a specific reason—the gazebo overlooked the An Jin wealth. Rows and rows of barley stretched before them. The outstanding view of undulating sheaves fed the misconception of her family's thriving coffers, though they had long since shriveled like these very fields on the cusp of winter.

"I run a plantation as well," he said. "Maize, planted in several towns across Teramaine."

"Oh?" Mailin asked, feigning surprise. She had chosen Vale Teranos over other high mages for the very reason that he was not only a lord of the province but one whose wealth came from farming.

She shot him an excessively bright smile. "My mamma used to help Father with his crop. She was key to enhancing much of his yield."

Vale's eyes gleamed with interest, though he kept his tone somber. "Ah, Jiiyi An Jin. Her reputation goes well beyond the borders. Even in Amereen, I've heard of her. I heard she died young and had not even seen a thousand turns of the sun."

Mailin dipped her head. "Yes, my lord."

He waved a gracious hand. "I am sorry. Let us speak of more pleasant things. Tell me, my dear, what manner of fae magic and mageborn ability do you yield?"

She turned to face the barley fields, choosing the words to keep her response vague. "I use Seelie magic whenever I heal"—she gave a flippant shrug—"but I have no specific mageborn ability, I'm afraid. I'm about as psychic as a human."

"Pity. Still, preternatural healing is an invaluable asset . . ." His fingers tapped on the wooden banister as he kept his gaze on the barley field. "What else can you do with Seelie magic?"

Nothing. Unlike her mother, Mailin couldn't use magic to influence the growth of plants. Much to her father's disappointment, healing was her only forte.

Vale didn't need to know that.

"My father's lands grow less fertile with every passing turn of the sun. It was my mother who kept his yields rich . . . After her passing, the crop yield dropped considerably." That, at least, was all truth. She glanced up, conjured a grin, and lied through her teeth. "So I stepped in."

From Vale's answering grin, she knew she'd fed him exactly what he wanted to hear. He had a pleasant smile, the sort that caused brackets in his cheeks and brought out a light in his eyes. "I cannot imagine why your father would wish to marry you off so soon."

Mailin sighed, carefully practiced before the mirror to reveal just the right amount of resignation. "Even Seelie magic can't stave off the increasing decline of his crop. Father reckons we are only delaying the inevitable, and he believes his lands should be fallow for some time before they can produce rich yield once more. A hard decision for him to make, but that is why he has offered my hand in marriage."

Vale issued a small, sympathetic hum. "Understandable. Your father was transparent in his correspondence and disclosed the manner of his finances. He even requested a small sum in exchange for your hand."

Mailin dipped her head as though shamed. "The taxes imposed upon us by our Lord Archmage Chikere are steep, and I am embarrassed to say that my father finds it hard to even afford my dowry . . ."

"I must confess, Lady An Jin, you are not what I was expecting."

Mailin mustered a coquettish smile. "What were you expecting?"

"From your father's correspondence . . ." He trailed off with a sheepish smile. "I admit, I had anticipated an unsightly maiden, too plain for pleasure, or perhaps a prudish termagant no other man wanted to claim."

Her lips twitched with genuine amusement. "Yet you came. Why would a lord such as yourself journey all the way here if you expected to be disappointed?"

He reached over to smooth her hair back, then tucked wayward strands behind her ear. Mailin stiffened but held herself still beneath his ministrations. He traced her skin from cheek to chin, raising chill bumps over her skin that had nothing to do with the cold. Or desire.

His grin widened as he fingered the tip of her ear, the subtle point a faint tribute to the Seelie blood flowing in her veins. "My dear, even if you were a disfigured harpy, I would be hard-pressed to turn down the opportunity to bring home a halfbreed to serve my liege's court."

"And what do you think now, my lord?" she asked, masking her indignation with a flirtatious smile.

He bent forward, so close that she inadvertently caught a whiff of his odor. She cringed inwardly. He smelled as though he'd bathed in ale and chewed on tobacco before rubbing a heavy dose of pomade over himself to mask the stench.

"I think you're proving to be well worth the effort"—he ran another liberal finger down the length of her arm, and Mailin fought the urge to slap it away—"provided you pass the tests, of course."

Mailin blinked. "What sort of tests?"

In response, he waved an arm to beckon someone as though

he were an archmage summoning his court.

In a few long-legged strides, the bondsman arrived at the gazebo, his form stiff and his eyes pointedly avoiding Mailin's face. "My lord?"

"Come here, Scar. Your assistance is required." Vale yanked a wicked-looking dagger from a hidden sheath in his boot.

Mailin's mouth went dry. "Wait. What are you doing?"

The smirk on Vale's face only deepened. The brackets on his cheeks suddenly appeared as cracks that revealed the cruelty beneath his charming facade. Before she could react, he struck swiftly and sank his dagger into his bondsman's abdomen.

Scar grunted, his features twisting in pain, yet he didn't put up any form of resistance. Not even when Vale yanked the dagger out again with a callous twist. Scar staggered back, clutching at the dark patch blooming on his stomach.

"Your first test, my dear."

With an inarticulate cry of shock, Mailin dashed to Scar's side and peeled up his tunic to access the weeping wound. Scar's breathing grew ragged as her fingers pressed over the puncture, which was too shallow to kill a mage, but deep enough to debilitate.

Healing required energy—magical or otherwise. While magic existed everywhere in nature, it was only accessible to the fae. Her Seelie roots gave her the ability to tap into some of it, and she drew as much as she could to channel into Scar's wound. However, a halfbreed's command of magic would never compare to that of a full-blooded fae. Mailin could never draw enough magic to completely heal a wound, so she usually bridged the gap with her own energy, which resulted in lethargy after a healing session.

When she removed her fingers, torn muscles had knitted back to smooth flesh. Her breaths came as pants from the amount of energy she'd expended. The only indication of Vale's mindless assault was a ripped tunic and blood-matted skin, but older scars snaked over the taut muscles on Scar's torso, indicating worse horrors he'd once suffered.

Mailin met the bondsman's gaze, fully expecting to see condemnation in those dark, haunted eyes. Instead, she saw unconcealed wonder. Scar stared at her with his lips slightly parted, very much reminiscent of the night before.

Applause severed their gaze. "Impressive," Vale murmured with a grin as he steepled his fingers together. "I have never seen a halfbreed heal, but that was *very* impressive. You would be a prize on the battlefield, my little dove."

Mailin clenched her fingers to stop her hands from trembling. "How could you do such a thing?" Vitriol filled her every word. More than anything, she loathed mindless acts of violence. "I could have demonstrated my ability with a simple nick of the knife. You didn't need to stab him!"

Vale laughed. Not a taunting smirk or a disparaging chuckle, but a deep guffaw borne of sheer amusement. "Scar's a tough bastard! That *was* a little nick for you, wasn't it, Scar?"

Scar gave a jerky nod, his jaw set in the hard edge of a man who knew better than to speak the truth. Mailin surged to her feet despite the fatigue stealing into her limbs. A firm hand gripped her wrist, stalling the expletive that almost exploded from the tip of her tongue.

Scar released her almost immediately, but she caught the warning in his eyes. "Thank you, my lady, but my lord was . . . prudent to test your abilities."

Vale rolled his eyes at the bondsman and gave him a dismissive wave. "You're done here. Leave us."

Scar climbed to his feet and gave a curt nod. With a final look of caution directed at Mailin, he turned and left, while she wrestled with her composure. Scar's pointed gaze had reminded her of her precarious position. She was speaking to a high mage, one she desperately needed in order to fulfill her own plans. Plans that were on the verge of ruin if she didn't keep her calm.

Expelling a breath, Mailin forced herself to turn back to Vale with a strained smile. She met his gaze, and her heart thudded at the predatory gleam there as he stared down at her with near lascivious approval.

"Well, my lord, have I passed the test?"

Another flash of teeth. "Absolutely, my dear. You are indeed remarkable. I will have the papers signed and the funds transferred to your father before week's end."

"About that, my lord," she began, biting into the insides of her cheek. "Would you still have me if I asked for an *increase* of the amount stipulated with my father?" The question left her lips before she could think better of it—borne from the part of her still incensed from his callous and cruel display. That part of her wanted to give him every chance to say no.

The high mage didn't appear surprised. Instead he merely shrugged. "How much more?"

"Double what you've agreed," she blurted.

Vale arched his brows, and Mailin quickly added, "As you know, I am my father's *only* daughter. Should I wed and reside in Amereen, he will be left all alone"—she feigned a sad smile—"and I worry ten thousand jaroobis may not be enough to tide him until his lands can be plowed again."

"Fret not, my dear." Vale waved a gracious hand. "Coin is of no consequence to me."

Mailin blinked. It was almost too easy. "Truly? You would pay twenty thousand jaroobis for my hand in marriage?"

He chuckled and leaned forward to catch a strand of her hair and boldly twirl it around his fingers. "My stallions are worth more than that, little dove."

She did not miss the implication that she was nothing more

to him than a thoroughbred mare, yet relief flooded over her like rain over dry cropland. One step closer to freedom.

"However, I must insist on one final test."

Her heart sank. "What is it?"

A lewd smirk lit his lips as he tugged her closer by yanking at her hair the way a rider would on a horse's reins. "You must assure me that you're no prudish termagant."

Mailin blinked, a flush creeping over her cheeks. Every fiber of her being itched to slap his hand away, to put distance between them. Instead, she took an obedient step forward as she replayed her mamma's last words in her mind.

"Leave, Mailin. You must find a way to leave this wretched place."

Vale Teranos was her only option.

Mailin squeezed her eyes shut as Vale backed her against the railing and tipped up her chin. His tongue prodded against her lips impatiently, seeking entry into her mouth. Vale's less than subtle pawing at her hips was a wild contrast to the gentle, near reverent way the bondsman had caressed her lips with his thumb.

Embarrassment heated her skin as she realized Scar was probably witnessing this very act. The thought caused her to stiffen, and she began pulling away. Vale gave her hair another insistent tug, hard enough to hurt.

Twenty thousand jaroobis.

She parted her lips and tried her best to inject enthusiasm into the kiss.

When he finally released her, he wore a wide grin. Relieved he didn't appear to find her performance disappointing, she offered him a wary smile, until his next words caused her to bite on her tongue.

"You're in sore need of tutoring, dove." A low chuckle. "I'll take great pleasure in teaching you how to please me."

FIVE

MAILIN

Vale insisted on a seafaring journey.

"The quicker we return to Amereen, the better," he had said with a suggestive smirk the moment her father had signed her betrothal papers.

Two days after her father had freed her from the unseen shackles of his possession, Mailin found herself aboard a grand three-masted barque, sailing the Southern Seas toward Amereen.

Curled on the wide sill of a tiny circular window in her cabin, Mailin stared out at the expanse of darkened waters stirring beneath the sulky night sky. At least Vale had afforded her the privacy of her own room. She grimaced. The choppy waves mirrored the roiling contents of her stomach.

Out of habit, her fingers slid across her collarbone into the inner folds of her grenadi until she found the embroidery. This one was of a swan, its wings stretched in flight. She rubbed her thumb carefully against the fraying stitches. She really ought to mend it, but she loathed to alter anything from her mother's hand.

She hummed the familiar lullaby, drawing comfort from the feel of her mother's embroidery until nausea gnawed in her belly.

Sighing, Mailin shuffled toward the pitcher on the small bedside table and poured herself a glass of water. She sipped slowly, trying to stave off the inevitable trudge she would soon have to make below deck to the galley for food. She wasn't sure she could keep even the water down.

She should not complain. Water sickness was a blessing in disguise.

Vale had made it patent he viewed her as a particularly fine piece of horseflesh he couldn't wait to ride. When he'd realized she couldn't keep the contents of her belly down, he had wanted nothing to do with her. For that, she was immeasurably grateful.

If luck stayed on her side, Mailin would execute the next step in her plans with her maidenhead intact and find a way to slip from his sight the moment they docked in Amereen's ports. She couldn't stay in Amereen, of course, not after such an outrageous con on its high mage. No, she would make her way north, past the borders into Batuhan. If her luck held, she'd look for the man they called the Curator, who was rumored to be a halfbreed. His specialty was helping people "disappear." She hadn't thought that far into her plan, but she'd find a way to either buy his service or convince him to help her.

Of course, she could have saved herself this entire ruse and run away from home years ago . . . had it not been for the promise that bound her to her father's side by the fae blood in her veins.

A flash of lightning split the skies, followed by another ominous boom of thunder. The ship rocked with an abrupt gusto that had Mailin dashing for the bucket to further drain her already empty stomach. A soft knock sounded at her door.

She gulped down some water before striding to the door and opened it warily, half expecting Vale to barge in. A briny mist flew at her face as the sky wept into the snarling seas.

Scar loomed before her, holding a wooden tray with a silver tureen and a covered breadbasket. Her stomach churned at the sight of food.

"My lady, you've not eaten anything all day." He hunched before the door, as though he were trying to shelter her from the spitting rain.

"I'm not hungry." She shifted on her feet, awkward like a newborn calf in his presence. He had afforded her nothing but politeness since their second encounter and had thankfully made no mention of their first.

"Come in," she added as rain began to fall in sheets around him. "You're getting wet."

He blinked, brows furrowing with obvious hesitation, but when she stood back in invitation, he strode in to place the tray on the tiny cabin table. He lingered there, and his towering presence seemed to shrink her cabin.

"I know you haven't been able to eat much, but I thought perhaps some broth . . ." He shrugged and reached into the back pocket of his breeches to pull out a tiny vial. "I . . . uh, also acquired some horshod from some of the sailors." He held out the vial. "They say the scent will help with the sickness."

Mailin uncorked the little bottle and took a quick sniff. The minty-medicinal scent of minced horshod leaves filled her nose. She'd administered many such tonics to expectant women suffering from nausea but had never thought of it as a remedy for water sickness. She clutched the vial to her chest, as warmth spread beneath her breastbone. "Thank you."

He grinned, and it wrought an uncanny change on his face, not to mention the fluttering within her ribcage. "You're very welcome, Lady An Jin." He took two backward steps toward the door before pausing. "Is there anything else I can do to make you feel better?"

It was her turn to grin. "Hmm . . . you could stop calling me that. Lady An Jin was my mother's title. My name is Mailin."

The corners of his lips lifted again, but this time it softened the rugged edges of his features into something that was almost shy. It was on the tip of her tongue to ask for his name—his *real* name—when the door slammed open, emitting a spray of rain and the shadow of a hulking man. Wind howled into the room until Vale kicked the door shut behind him.

"There you are." He stalked in, water dripping from his clothes to puddle on the wooden planks. Mailin took an uneasy step back. Hardness suffused his tone, his usual charm tainted with a callous edge.

Scar moved forward as though to intercept him. "Vale, one of the sailors informed me of a gambling round this eve. Shall we leave Lady An Jin to her dinner and join the crew below deck?"

Mailin frowned. Over the days on the ship, she'd noticed a peculiar dynamic between the two. Not only did Scar behave more like a chief steward than a lowly bondsman, but he was afforded liberties such as the use of his master's given name.

Vale shrugged off his arm, his lips a thin line. "I doubt that. The sudden storm has the crew frantic. Besides, why gamble when there are more . . . pleasurable ways to spend my time?"

Mailin stiffened.

"Vale," Scar said. His head dipped to reflect his subservience, though his tone remained insistent. "Lady An Jin isn't well."

Vale rolled his eyes. "Oh, piss off."

The bondsman tensed, the muscles on his arms cording visibly. "Vale—"

Vale narrowed his eyes, and with a flick of his wrist, Scar slammed to the ground as though shoved by an invisible hand.

Mailin bit down on her lips to muffle her shock. Her heart pounded frenetically in her chest. She had known Vale was telekinetic, but she had never imagined him quite so *strong*. Telekinesis was a common mageborn ability. While most could easily move small objects with their mind, it was a rare feat for a mage to move a man the size of Scar—much less pin him to the ground.

Vale sneered. "*Get out.*"

Scar pushed from the ground, his gaze darting from Vale to Mailin, who remained frozen on her feet.

"What?" Vale asked with a lewd twist of his lips. "Are you hoping for another show? I may share whores, but this is my *bride*."

There was a subtle darkening of Scar's eyes, and a not-so-subtle clenching of his fists. In response, Vale took a threatening step forward. Despite the sickness rioting in her belly, Mailin placed a hand on her betrothed's arm before he could dole out another psychic punch.

"That's enough," she said, amazed by the steadiness of her own voice. "Scar, thank you for the horshod and my dinner tray but . . . you should leave us."

Scar glanced at her for a taut moment, a muscle tightening prominently in his temple. Then he turned and stormed from the cabin, shutting the door behind him with a dull thud like a death knell.

Mailin turned to find Vale watching her with an indeterminate expression. "Tell me, my dear. What was Scar doing in your room?"

Seeking to gather her wits, she walked over to the small dresser and poured two glasses of water, taking the time to settle her nerves before she responded. "As I said, he delivered my dinner, and a paste to help with my water sickness."

She held out a second glass to Vale.

"Did he?" Vale intoned with his arms folded, pointedly

ignoring her offering. "How very thoughtful of him."

Mailin frowned. "Vale . . ."

"A hundred and twelve summers," Vale said. "That is how long he's served me. And I have never once seen him look at a woman the way he looks at *you*."

Mailin parted her lips.

"I . . ." She clamped her mouth shut. What should she say? She couldn't possibly reveal that in all *her* life, she had never felt as attracted to a man either—a man who was *not* her betrothed.

Perhaps Vale was also telepathic. As though enraged by her wayward thoughts, he knocked the glass from her hand. The glass splintered in a hail of shards and water.

He grabbed a handful of her hair, looping the strands in his fist as he yanked her close. "Let me remind you, little dove," he said, his last word no longer an endearment but a taunt. "Scar serves me. Just as you will serve me."

He shoved her onto the cabin's small bed. "And I will be damned if I am to be cuckolded by my own slave."

"Vale!" Mailin scrambled off the bed. "You're mistaken. I've not been unfaithful. I—"

He pinned her down easily, his breath hot in her ear. His hand clamped over her neck in a wholly threatening gesture. "Then lie back and show me."

She yanked at his wrists. "You said there would be a Promise Ceremony!"

Vale laughed. "A Promise Ceremony doesn't require the bride to be a virgin, now does it? I paid for you." He yanked the length of her grenadi from her shoulders and tore at her koshiyin wrap. "Show me what I've paid so handsomely for."

For a moment, she lay perfectly still, paralyzed by terror. Her machinations had led her to this moment. She had put herself in this situation. Vale shoved aside her loosened wrap to grope at her bare flesh, and the invasion of his touch wrenched a shriek from her throat.

She clawed and bucked at the same time the ship tilted, and the combined motion knocked Vale to the floor, where he sprawled, legs akimbo.

Mailin glimpsed the handle of the dagger he kept in the side of his boot. Without hesitation, she snatched it from its sheath.

Vale righted himself and narrowed his gaze at the dagger in her hand. "You wouldn't *dare*."

Mailin gritted her teeth. "Try me."

Vale made to lunge for her at the same time the cabin door burst open.

Scar filled the doorway. "Vale, stop."

Only then did Mailin realize she'd slashed Vale across the chest in her panic—an ugly streak of red spread across the white silk of his shirt in time with the dread manifesting as icicles in her gut. Goddess of mercy, she had bled her betrothed. A *high mage*.

She ought to beg forgiveness. Offer to heal. Instead, she scrambled from the bed, her heart pounding at the murderous rage in Vale's expression. She'd seen that look on a man before. Father had donned it often, and it *never* boded well for Mamma. She darted to the door, then halted. Scar's forbidding frame barred her escape. She curled her fingers around the dagger still clutched in her hands and shot him a beseeching glance.

"Come back here, you little bitch!" Vale snarled.

Scar's lips flattened.

Her knees nearly buckled with relief when he backed away from the door. Like a mouse sprung from a trap, she streaked through the doorway while Vale's curses blistered the air.

Mailin fled through the narrow aisle, her heart pounding in her ears, her bare feet slipping as she ran toward the starboard deck. Rain lashed against her skin in punishing streaks.

Some of the crew stared at her in open curiosity, their eyes widening at the dagger in her hand, but most paid her no heed as they bustled about the sails. Mailin skidded, losing her balance on the spume-licked deck, nearly dropping the dagger. She tucked the weapon, her only fulcrum for security, into her belt.

"Railea is raging across the seas, my lady! Return to your cabin," shouted a nearby deckhand. He was fastening the knots to a small dinghy. The wooden lifeboat swayed hard enough in the wind that it hammered against the ship's hull.

Help me, she wanted to scream, but she only managed to shake her head like a mute as the wild wind tugged strands of her hair and the waves howled their ire. The deckhand cast her a disapproving frown before another sailor called him away.

Mailin edged toward the starboard deck, where the dinghy was secured. It swayed ominously, hanging from the side of the ship like an untucked tunic. Did she *dare*? She cast another peek over the wooden railing, and whatever confidence she'd had withered. The sky and sea melded together in an expanse of unending gray, a terrifying tempest threatening to swallow her whole. Her nausea returned with a vengeance.

"Where do you think you're going?"

Mailin sucked in a breath of brine before she swiveled around to Vale's thunderous countenance boring down at her. Her heart sank.

Scar was nowhere in sight.

Most of the crew was too frantic to notice, and those who did made no move to aid her. No one in their right mind would defy a high mage. No one was going to help her.

"I'm sorry," she cried. "I didn't mean to—"

"Oh, you'll *be* sorry," Vale said with a malicious snarl. "Now get back to the damned cabin!"

Mailin flinched from the blatant command in his tone. She

hadn't traded freedom from under her father's thumb only to be oppressed by another man. That had never been part of her plan, and if that was to be her fate, she would rather take her chances with the sea.

Decision made, Mailin yanked up her skirts and flung herself over the railing, right into the dinghy. It swung like a pendulum with her sudden weight.

Vale's shout sliced through the storm. "Hellion! What do you think you're doing?"

Mailin tugged at the central bowline mooring the dinghy to the hull. Another wave crested, causing the ship to yaw erratically while a splash of cold seawater doused her from head to hem. It only spurred her action.

"Cease your foolishness!" Vale shouted from the deck. "You'll drown, you madwoman!"

Despite the fear fisting in her heart, Mailin glared up at her betrothed. She had never been one for obedience. She retrieved her hidden dagger and hacked at the bowline, trying to cut through the thick cords.

Not her best plan. Vale screamed expletives, and an aberrant force wrapped around her, nearly hauling her off her feet. Vale was attempting to *lift* her with his mind. The dinghy swayed in protest as Mailin tightened her grip and sawed erratically.

Blast it, the rope was a lot thicker than she'd imagined, and the dagger suddenly seemed like a butter knife.

"My lady!" Scar appeared abruptly by the handrail, blood smeared beneath his nose. "You won't best the storm!" He leaned over the railing with an outstretched hand. "Take my hand! Please, I won't let him hurt you."

As the last word left his lips, a huge wave mounted to crash into the dinghy. The ship lurched with such violence that Mailin staggered with a shriek. The dagger slipped from her hands. Water weighed down her skirts, and saltwater stung her vision. She took an unsteady step back. Her shin hit a wooden bench. She stumbled, arms windmilling for balance.

A loud *snap.*

It wasn't until she slammed against a hard, wooden edge that she realized the entire dinghy had fallen clear from the ship and plummeted.

Straight into the sea.

SIX

KILLIAN

"No!" Killian lunged forward as the wooden boat bearing the woman plunged into the water. "*Mailin!*"

Horror squeezed his chest so tightly that he struggled to breathe. He couldn't even tell if she was conscious. All he could see was a speck of scarlet curled within a tiny boat that could be swallowed by the sea at any moment.

Killian whirled to Vale. "Why did you do that?"

Instead of lifting Mailin up to safety, the high mage had inadvertently caused the entire dinghy to crash with his brutish use of telekinesis.

"I was only trying to haul her up," Vale protested, more flustered than Killian had ever seen him.

"So do something!" Killian roared when Vale did nothing but stare.

"I—I can't!" he yelled, a man who rarely admitted any weakness. "The boat's too heavy and she's too far."

Even Vale's mastery of telekinesis was limited by range.

"Release me." Killian jerked at the collar around his neck. "I'll get her."

Fury and indecision twisted Vale's features before he finally spat out his decision. "No."

Killian clenched his fists. "I can do it. You know I can."

"*No.*" The vehemence in Vale's voice was one Killian was familiar with—whenever the high mage made up his mind, there was no changing it.

Killian yanked off his boots.

"Don't you dare!" Vale snarled. "Scar!"

Without giving the high mage a response, he swung himself over the railing, and flinging his body as far as he could from the hull, dove headfirst into the water.

Rain lashed her face like tiny unforgiving whips while saltwater stung her eyes and brine burned in her throat. The waves were far choppier than she'd expected and her dinghy bobbed with the erraticism of a toy boat in a child's tub.

She clutched at the oar, curling her fingers tight over this one. She had already lost the other, unprepared for the roughness of the waves that had torn it from her grip. The ship grew smaller as the waves dragged her farther and farther. The sea howled, unforgiving in its wild and watery fury as it hurled her dinghy this way and that. She tried in vain to paddle, but dimly realized she didn't know *where* to go. She would be lucky to stay afloat. How had she thought this was a better option than facing Vale?

Something tugged on the side of the boat. Wild panic seized her. Thoughts of sea serpents and the kraken loomed in her mind. The dinghy bobbled, tipping precariously to one side as an *arm* reached up from the water and latched onto the side of the boat.

A dark head emerged from the surface, an unearthly silhouette backlit by lightning forking in the raging skies.

Vale!

Swinging back with all her might, Mailin aimed her oar at the rising head. It connected with a *crack*, and the resulting yelp had her gasping.

Not the high mage. *Scar!*

Mailin lurched forward and grabbed a fistful of his shirt before he could slip off the side of the boat. Somehow, he managed to keep his grip on the side of the craft, and with a powerful lunge, he clambered aboard.

"I'm sorry," she shouted over the wind whipping her hair. "I didn't know it was you!"

He paid her no heed. His gaze fixed on something beyond her shoulder. Lightning speared the skies again, illuminating the fear in his eyes, turning her blood to ice. She didn't have a chance to turn before the impact sent her hurtling headlong into the dark waters.

Killian groaned. Searing brightness assaulted his vision, and pain assailed the side of his ribs. He blinked and squinted, trying to regain his bearings. He lay prone on his chest. The ground was gritty and damp, and a cool wetness pooled around his feet. He dragged in a deep breath only to cough as he inhaled bits of sand in the process.

He lifted his head, a groan leaking from his throat. The beach stretched endlessly, a rolling golden strip hugged by buoyant waves of glittering turquoise. The sun lounged high in the cloudless sky, as though the storm had been nothing but a torrid nightmare.

The *storm*. The boat crashing into a cluster of rocks. Mailin's terrified screams.

He bolted up, scrambling to his knees. *Mailin.* Where was she?

Pain needled at his ribs. Killian lifted his sodden tunic to find a smattering of bruises and lacerations that had already begun to scab, indicating he'd been unconscious for longer than he'd thought. The ache at the bottom left of his rib indicated some form of fracture. No real damage. At least, nothing he was unaccustomed to. Ignoring his injuries, he scanned the expanse of untouched sand.

No one in sight for miles.

They had to have been close to land to begin with if the dinghy had crashed into rocks. If he had been washed to shore, the current would have likely dragged Mailin here, too.

Killian gritted his teeth. He'd had her in his arms for a fleeting moment until the sea had wrenched her from his grasp. Then he'd slammed into something hard—likely more rocks—and lost consciousness altogether.

He blew out a breath.

Blasted Vale! Had he taken off his collar, this could all be avoided. Clearly, Mailin had been of less value to the high mage than Killian's indenture. Now he was stranded on some gods-forgotten beach, and she was lost.

Was she lying somewhere at the bottom of the ocean right now? A pang struck his chest at the thought, throbbing worse than the ache in his ribs. Killian grabbed at his temples with a groan when a distinctly feminine scream strangled all sound from his lips.

He pushed up from his knees, his feet sinking into damp sand. The beach stretched endlessly like a giant serpent sunning itself beside the water, its tail curling near the horizon as the island curved from view. Only the constant shush of waves permeated the deceptively tranquil silence. Had Mailin's scream been his imagination?

Another distant shout shot adrenaline through his veins. He sprinted, his bare feet squelching into the sand as waves tugged at his feet. He hurtled down the shoreline, searching for the source of the sound, and picked up speed when he heard low laughter. Raucous and malicious and male.

From the distance, he made out five silhouettes. Four men chasing a smaller, unmistakably feminine figure. In a red dress. A thousand needles prickled his skin, a long-forgotten itch to *warp*, restricted only by the collar that burned around his neck.

Another scream spliced through the air. Killian pumped his feet harder as he streaked across the sand, his heart lurching in his chest.

Eight hundred paces away. Mailin ran doggedly down the shore in the opposite direction. The men laughed again, circling her like hungry wolves as they corralled her to the shoreline.

Six hundred paces away. The largest of the four lunged. He yanked at her ankles and jerked her to the ground. She fell to the sand. Her cries spurred Killian like a whip, stoking a mindless rage in his chest.

Four hundred paces away. A lanky man whose stringy hair hung well past his shoulders pinned Mailin's arms while the first man straddled her. The other two circled like avid vultures. One even snuck his hands into his pants, palming himself as he leered. Mailin's shouts turned to a litany of incomprehensible shrieks, unwittingly damning the men to bloody deaths.

Two hundred paces away. Killian issued a guttural roar, and all heads swiveled in his direction. When he intended to kill, he made sure his marks saw it coming.

He reached for the nearest man. A pasty-skinned redhead with a wiry build. The man barely had his hand out of his pants before Killian's knuckles connected with his face. Bones crunched beneath his fist.

In the split second before Redhead slumped, Killian noted two things. The men all had a glowing symbol tattooed at the side of their throats, and they carried pickaxes, strapped to their backs on makeshift baldrics.

"Who the fuck are you?" asked the stockiest man of the lot, his brows crawling together like a pair of bushy caterpillars.

Killian grasped the pickaxe from the now-unconscious Redhead's back and struck out. Bushy Brows ducked before he was impaled in the head, a near-soundless gasp escaping his throat. Killian slammed Redhead's limp frame in Bushy Brows's direction and they collapsed in a tangle of limbs.

The man who'd been straddling Mailin jumped to his feet with a snarl to charge Killian like a heckled steer in a bullring. Killian waited until the man had committed to a tackle before dodging swiftly out of the way.

The dim-witted bull didn't have a chance to evade before Killian buried the pickaxe in his back. He bared his teeth—*he'd missed the spine*—but the bull dropped to his knees in a roar of pain.

"Paddy!" shouted the one still holding Mailin captive by her wrists. He gaped at his comrade, who was attempting the grisly act of removing the pickaxe from his back, gouging his own flesh as fresh blood spurted.

Mailin's eyes were wide and wild as she cried, "Behind you!"

Killian wrenched the pickaxe free, eliciting another howl from Paddy before he embedded it again—into Bushy Brows' head. The man wore an expression of shock even as he slumped into a heap on the sand, the curved edge of the pickaxe splitting his skull right between his unruly brows.

Mailin's captor belted out a furious stream of expletives, stringy hair obscuring his face as he shoved her to the sand. He fumbled at his belt. Sunlight glinted briefly over his weapon, enough for Killian to make out a blade. Stringy charged, slashing wildly.

Bloody amateur.

Killian sidestepped the mindless attack with ease, pivoted, and used the man's momentum to shove him into the sand.

He pounced on Stringy's back and grabbed the man's head with both hands. Twisted with all his might. A satisfying crack sounded before Stringy crumpled, nothing more than a clump of seaweed washed ashore.

"Scar—" Mailin's shout barely registered before heavy arms tackled him from behind. They crashed to the warm sand in a grappling heap.

"I'll boil your brains to broth and have it after I'm done with her!" Spittle flew as Paddy roared, blue veins bulging at his temples. Despite the wound to his back, the man hurled *solid* punches. For a moment, Killian only defended himself while he admired his opponent's form . . . until Paddy landed a blow to his head and pinpricks of white exploded across his vision.

Time to end it.

A well-aimed punch to Paddy's abdomen only fueled the man's fury. The bastard was so heavily muscled, Killian barely made a dent. Paddy hurled another punch and pain blazed across his skull.

Killian grunted. He rammed his knuckles up into the fleshiest part of Paddy's throat, causing his opponent to wheeze. Killian reared up to wrap an arm over his adversary's neck and haul the man closer. Clamping Bull's throat within the crook of his elbow, he squeezed. Hard. Paddy pummeled Killian with punches, garbled screams spewing from his lips as he began to choke.

Paddy halted abruptly. His lips parted like a gasping fish before he fell over with a heavy thump.

A small, pale face with frantic eyes peered down at him.

Killian blew out a breath.

Mailin had impaled Paddy in the back.

"G-goddess of light, I . . . I k-killed," she said. "I k-killed a man."

Killian didn't offer her any comfort. In fact, he all but shoved her aside. Mailin's gasp resounded in his ears as he bolted to his knees, sprinting after Redhead. Somewhere along the way, he'd awoken. And the coward was tearing toward the forest covering.

Killian caught up to the man and slammed him to the ground. "Please," Redhead cried, sheltering his head with skinny arms.

His pleas slicked over Killian like grease. All he saw was Redhead palming himself as Paddy straddled a shrieking Mailin on the ground.

Another punch satisfied the rage still boiling his blood. He wrapped his hands around the bastard's head and twisted until Redhead stilled and sagged.

Killian drew in a steadying breath, scrutinizing the tree line to make sure there were no other witnesses before turning back toward the beach.

She was still on her feet, a disheveled figure wrapped in scarlet and shock.

"Mailin." Her name slipped from his lips in a growl. Adrenaline still coursed through his veins. He would have taken her into his arms if she hadn't backed away, fear etched into every line of her face.

"Don't come any closer." She brandished the bloody knife.

The steadiness of her voice and the vehemence in her tone could almost fool Killian—if her hands weren't shaking.

He gentled his voice. "I'm not going to hurt you."

"Don't come any closer," she repeated. "Or I'll kill you, too."

SEVEN

MAILIN

Mailin kept the knife trained at Scar even though relief beat through her bones at the sight of him. Logic told her he had never done anything to hurt her, but her fear was not a logical thing. Four bodies were strewn across the sand, but he didn't even appear winded. In fact, apart from the purpling bruises on the side of his face, he didn't look any worse for the wear.

Her aggressors had never stood a chance.

Mailin hadn't understood why a lord, a high mage, had chosen to travel with only *one* bondsman for company. Now she did.

He stepped forward, and Mailin jumped back. "Stop!" she said, waving the knife with as much menace as she could. "I mean it."

His gaze shifted from her to the weapon in her hands, and the corners of his mouth twitched.

His amusement stiffened her spine. She didn't believe for one minute she could stop him, either, but she wouldn't allow him to believe her helpless. He might have saved her from a terrible fate, but as far as she knew, a bondsman's loyalty to his lord was absolute.

"I'm not going to hurt you," he repeated, his voice a reassuring rumble. He extended his arms and took a step forward. She shrank back.

Frustration flickered over his features.

"Lady An Jin," he said, as though trying to recompose himself by reverting to the use of her formal title. "I need you to trust me." He stretched out a hand, and she shied to the side. He advanced again, but she darted away, determined to keep at least three paces of distance between them. With their gazes locked, they continued in this strange, silent dance until the waves lapped at her feet.

"Why did you come after me?" she demanded. "What do you want from me?"

His brows pinched. He stared at her as though she were daft. "To keep you *safe*. Right now, I'd like to see to that wound on your head."

Mailin blinked and touched the side of her throbbing temple, where her hair was plastered to her skin. Her fingers came away smeared with red. Railea's breath, she was bleeding. No wonder her head pounded.

Only when his fingers clamped over her wrist did she realized she'd foolishly allowed herself to be distracted. She released a cry before his other hand clamped over her mouth with terrifying strength.

"*Shhh!*" His voice filled her ears. "Calm down. I'm not going to hurt you, but these men likely belong to a larger group. We do not want to draw any more attention."

She nodded.

He held her gaze for another moment, as though to ascertain her calm, before he slowly loosened his grip.

"There's a good girl," he murmured. "Now, hold still."

Relief crashed over her when he didn't attempt to pry the knife from her grip—trusting her not to hurt him. Instead, his gaze wandered to her temple. Gentle hands probed at her head, stroking her hair back as though she were a child.

He grimaced before saying, "Not too deep. Needs to be cleaned, but it should heal on its own soon enough." He frowned. "Can you heal yourself?"

Mailin shook her head, acutely aware of the proximity of his large body, of the streaks of sand, sweat, and blood glistening on his forearms. He wasn't as large as the man who had pinned her to the sand, but he was twice as intimidating with the scars lacerating his face. And the tightly corded muscles of his frame had proven to be twice as deadly. Yet the last of her fear melted away, adrenaline ebbing from her system so swiftly that sudden lightheadedness assailed her. She was also painfully conscious of her parched throat.

Her grip on the knife loosened. "I can't use magic on myself."

"That's a pity," he said. "Are you hurt anywhere else?"

At the tender concern in his tone, an enormous sob escaped her throat. His eyes widened. She couldn't fathom her unspeakable fate had he not shown up when he did. A violent shudder wracked her body, and he pulled back to study her face.

"My lady . . . ?"

The knife slipped from her fingers and to the sand as she emitted another sob, unable to control the bone-deep tremor traveling through her marrow. She buried her face in his chest in a desperate attempt to conceal the deluge building behind her eyes. Something about him made her feel precious, as though she would be protected at all costs—so she allowed herself to sob. Loud, ugly sobs where she spewed tears and made whistling noises through her nose. A foolish thing, considering her growing thirst. Yet she had no words to express her gratitude, no words to make sense of the emotion he inflicted with his gruff voice and gentle hands.

The bondsman held himself stiff as driftwood as she soaked his already damp shirtfront. She had come so close to living the horrors she'd worked so hard to escape.

The tension eventually left his body. His arms wrapped around her, cradling her like a child as he murmured platitudes in her ear, which only stoked more tears.

She didn't know how long she clung to him, but when her sobs finally ebbed to sniffling hiccups, he lifted her chin. His thumb stroked the edge of her jaw, a motion that reminded her of their brief encounter in the alleyway. Her cheeks warmed.

Mailin wrenched from his hold and ducked her head, suddenly mortified. The last time she'd cried like this had been when Mamma died. Even then, she'd bawled in the privacy of her own bedchamber, unseen and unheard by anyone.

"You're all right," he said with more conviction than was warranted. "I won't let anyone hurt you." Mailin bit hard on her bottom lip. No one had said those words to her since Mamma had passed.

"Who were they?" she asked.

He studied the corpses with his mouth set in a grim slash.

"Judging from this . . ." He bent down to trace the symbol etched into one of the necks, glowing even on the corpse.

Mailin blinked at the markings that had escaped her notice. "The *rune of revocation*?"

Every mage feared this. The rune of revocation was the ultimate punishment, seared into the skin by one of the Echelon of Archmages. Not only did it mark the individual for life, but it also acted as a more permanent version of the bondsman's metal collar— it stripped all forms of mageborn ability from the individual.

"I think we're on Groydon." He gave a dismal shake of his

head, and his words held such an ominous edge that the hair on her arms stood on end even as an involuntary hiccup escaped her throat. "Where?"

"The Isle of Groydon," he said.

Mailin had never been outside of Jachuana. Gods, the seedy alleyways of Jirin's whorehouses were the furthest she'd ever wandered from the sphere of the manor grounds.

"Is it a part of Amereen?"

Scar released a snort. "The Isle of Groydon is not precisely a *part* of Amereen as much as it is under the governance of its archmage, Lord Thorne."

She continued to stare at him blankly.

He raised his brows, which stretched the scar on his face in a way that made her fingers itch to stroke. "Does the name Prison Island mean anything to you?"

"*Prison Island*?" Her forehead wrinkled at the prosaic term even as her lips parted. "The place where all Amereen's criminals are sent?"

"Criminals?" Scar shook his head with a short bark of laughter. "Criminals usually serve out their sentences the way the Circle of High Mages see fit. This place is reserved for the truly . . . depraved."

"Truly depraved?" she repeated like a demented parrot as fear grew in her chest. She recalled the zealous, pitiless eyes of her attackers, and her breath shortened. "You mean murderers, rapists, and such?"

Scar gave another shake of his head. "I once heard of a farmer who'd murdered his own wife. Killed her in a drunken rage, all because his dinner had run cold."

Incredulity loosened her jaw. "Was he sentenced here?"

"The Circle sentenced him to death. This place . . . most of the offenders are sentenced here by the Lord Archmage Thorne himself." He paused. "Only men who commit truly wicked offenses are sent here."

Mailin could only blink. If a man who'd murdered his own wife for serving him cold food was not considered *truly* wicked, what had the other men done to be sent here?

"How do we get out of this place?" She wrung her hands, but the blood staining her fingers drew her gaze, reminding her of the murder she'd just committed. Goddess of light, she'd just *killed*. The enormity of the fact reared like a ravenous beast, ready to devour. Mailin drew in a long, shuddering breath and wrestled it into the back of her mind. There were far more terrifying matters at hand. Like being marooned on a place called Prison Island, which was apparently *too good* for wife killers. "Surely . . . surely, we can appeal to the guards. Explain how we got here."

Scar rubbed a hand against his temple, as though he were suffering a particularly bad bout of migraine. "As far as I know, there are no guards on this island. The prisoners may be sentenced here by the archmage, but the only way to leave it is through death."

EIGHT

KILLIAN

The little temptress gaped at Killian as though he'd sprouted two heads. She shook her head, denial and dread filling her eyes before she gestured at a piece of driftwood dragged up to the shore by dancing waves.

"We can make a raft or something," she said in a thin, desperate voice. "The storm has passed. We'll be better off taking our chances at sea."

"The isle is warded, my lady. Else the prisoners would have escaped the moment they arrived." He'd wager his life the wards around Groydon were designed to imprison and most likely fatal if breached.

Her shock ebbed only to be replaced by indignant anger. "How in Railea's name did we end up ashore if it was warded?"

Having lived in the enclave, Killian knew wards more intimately than an average civilian. "Wards don't keep people from coming in, my lady. It keeps those within from going out." Like a fish trap.

She sputtered. "We're not criminals! Whoever cast these wards must realize we've landed here by mistake!"

Killian frowned. He wasn't entirely sure how an archmage's wards worked. Perhaps she was right. Perhaps the archmage did sense their sudden intrusion. But would he *care*?

"And Vale," she added, her voice faltering. "Wouldn't he . . . search for us?"

Killian swallowed the anger that rose from the mention of the high mage. "Likely." Vale *would*—he wouldn't give Killian up so easily. Yet it would be foolish to expect a search party from Vale. The high mage couldn't know where the tides had carried them.

Killian sighed. "What matters right now is for us to leave before we encounter more of the island's inhabitants." He didn't hasten to add the worst of his fears—the inhabitants had likely not seen a woman for a *long* time. As far as he'd heard, no female— mage or human—had been sentenced to Groydon.

Mailin nodded her agreement with downturned lips.

"Come," he said, taking her by the forearm. The slightness of her hand unnerved him. So small she was, she hardly came up to his chin. His stomach churned at the thought of what would have happened to her had he drowned at sea.

She shook off his grasp to pick up the sodden ends of her grenadi. It had fallen off her shoulders to lay like a rumpled red snake on the beach. Killian swallowed as he stared briefly at her bare shoulders covered in scratches and sand. Fortunately, the white strip she wore like a bandage around her chest kept her decent. Though the lengthy garment appeared heavy. How much must it weigh now that it was drenched with seawater?

"A wonder you survived the waters clad in this attire."

"I managed to latch onto a part of the dinghy. It had turned on its end, but the fabric actually helped me hang once I climbed up. I was plastered over the boards like some obstinate octopus."

Killian grunted because he couldn't formulate an intelligible response. He was just relieved she was alive and relatively unscathed.

She cast a critical eye over her fallen attackers and surprised him by shuffling over to where Redhead lay in a heap in the sand. She glanced back at Killian almost nervously before she said, "Will you help me?"

Killian closed the distance with a frown. "With what?"

"Help me . . . undress him." She crouched beside the body.

Killian blinked, uncertain if he'd heard her right. When he understood her intentions, a huff of laughter wound up his throat.

"You want his clothes?"

She flattened her lips and gestured at the crumpled ends of the dress in her hands. "How far do you think I can go dressed in this?"

The lady made a fair point.

Killian made quick work of stripping the corpse of its garments. When he removed Redhead's pants, he didn't miss her reddening cheeks and dipped chin. Practical but innocent. He smirked until he remembered whom she belonged to, then he sobered, the curve of his lip becoming a firm line. Vale would soon stamp out all forms of purity.

"Here," he said, rolling up the garments and handing them to her.

"Thank you." She took the clothes from him gingerly and held them up for inspection. She brought it to her nose for a quick sniff and her features contorted in disgust.

Killian was aching and weary and parched for water, yet mirth twitched his lips. When she met his gaze with a scowl, he cleared his throat. Clearly unimpressed with his amusement at her expense, she rose jerkily to her feet and tilted her chin in the most adorable manner. She stalked toward the tree line marked by gnarled roots protruding in coarse sand.

"Where are you going?"

She paused and gave him a sidelong glare. "To fix my hair." She sniffed. "Where do you think? I'm going to find a place to change."

"No wandering off. We don't know where these men came from."

She sucked in an audible breath. "Then where can I—"

"Here," he said.

Her brows lifted, causing heat to burn at the back of his neck.

"I won't look." He promptly turned to his back to prove his point. "Just be quick about it."

Silence, followed by a long-suffering sigh. Then he heard shuffling skirts. After a moment, more silence reigned. He counted three crashing waves before he began to wonder if she had stealthily fled up the dunes behind his back.

"Lady An Jin?"

A distinct rustling. "Don't turn around!"

Killian shook his head. "We really ought to get moving."

"Do you know how hard it is to undo wet bindings?" she countered, followed by the sound of more swishing. "Have you ever tried unlacing a grenadi tied to a koshiyin wrapped around you five times?"

The heat burning his neck rose to warm his ears. She had unknowingly conjured visions of him unravelling the white band from her curves. Killian rubbed the back of his neck. He should not be entertaining such thoughts. She was a lady, soon to be Lady Teranos. Killian clenched his jaw. *Vale's* lady.

Annoyed, he groused. "Are you done?"

She made a noise that mirrored his own frustration. "I suppose."

Killian turned around and swallowed. Hard. He blinked, trying not to stare. Somehow, she had managed to make a dead man's attire provocative. Redhead's leather pants molded to her thighs, outlining the gentle flare of her hips and her shapely legs.

Killian dragged his gaze from her hips to her top.

Railea's blood! Why was the linen so thin?

He hadn't thought much of the shirt until she'd donned it, but now, the fabric somehow teased over her skin, accentuating the softness of her shoulders and the swell of her . . . Killian pinned his gaze firmly to her face. He swallowed again.

She had released the pins in her hair. Her damp locks were disheveled, gossamer strands of soot lifted by the breeze to dance around the fine bones of her face. She truly looked like a doll. A very sensual one.

"What? Do I look utterly ridiculous?" she asked with a tiny pucker between her brows.

Ridiculous? At this rate, she would soon drive him insane.

He managed a grunt, averting his eyes. "The shirt is a little sheer."

She gasped and folded protective arms over her chest. Struck by sudden ingenuity, Killian shrugged off his own shirt.

When he held it out to her, *she* was the one who couldn't seem to stop staring. Warmth heated his face. He knew what she was staring at. His scars were not limited to his face, and his body was a sight most women shied away from—exactly why he never took his clothes off around one.

"Try this," he said, trying not to squirm when her gaze tracked the crisscrossing lines mapping his torso. "My shirt might be . . . thicker," he finished lamely.

She surprised him by accepting his offer just as he was about to withdraw his arm. "Thank you. But what . . ." She pressed his shirt against her chest. "What about you?"

Killian nodded at the bodies strewn closer to the shore. "One of them will fit me."

He turned around, cringing at the view she must have of his bare back, which bore the worst of his scars. After all, the guardians had started there until his back healed in ropy welts that desensitized him to the burn of the blade. And like morbid painters out of canvas space, they progressed to his chest, his abdomen, his face.

Swallowing painful memories long past, he jogged over to Bull's corpse and stripped off the man's linen shirt. It was threadbare and tattered, but as long as it protected him from the glare of the sun and kept his mangled skin hidden, it would serve him fine.

A thick, leather baldric covered the corpse beneath the shirt. Killian rolled the body to its front and found a waterskin strapped to the body's flank. He shook it, pleased to hear the sloshing contents. He'd have to check the other corpses for waterskins. Killian undid the cork and swigged a mouthful.

Bliss.

He defied the urge to drain the waterskin, saving the rest for the little temptress. He hung the strap over his shoulder and began relieving the corpse of its boots. No sense wasting good shoes when Killian's own feet were bare, and Bull's were large enough to fit him comfortably.

He was lacing up his new footwear when Mailin shouted, "Scar!"

Killian swiveled back to see Mailin flying toward him, kicking up tiny sand clouds as she ran. The silhouettes of two men emerged from the tree line.

Fuck.

He met Mailin halfway and shoved her behind himself as he narrowed his eyes at the two newcomers. They stared at the bodies strewn on the sand, shock evident on their faces.

The taller of the pair uttered something incoherent before he scrambled toward Stringy's corpse. The second man's gaze roved to the body at Killian's feet, whose shoes he had just stolen. "Padric!"

Stunned eyes locked on him. "Blazing hellfires, *you* killed Eyeball Paddy?"

Killian held up both hands in a gesture of peace as he took a step forward. "We were defending ourselves," he said, calculating the quickest and quietest way of ending the pair.

At his words, the man caught sight of Mailin. His eyes widened even more, staring at her as though she were a siren fresh from the sea.

The taller one looked up from Stringy's corpse, his eyes glassy. "My *brother*. That's my brother!" He howled before he charged, fists flying. "I'm going to pick my teeth with your bones!"

Killian didn't hesitate.

He wrenched the pickaxe from the sand beside Padric's corpse. It was easy to take a man down when he was driven by rage and not rationality. In less than three seconds, his attacker slumped to the ground with bits of indeterminate gore spewing from the side of his head the pickaxe had cracked open.

The second man fled in the direction of the tree line. Killian charged after him. He had to neutralize the threat before the man returned with his friends. A weak shout from behind slowed his steps. Killian bit back a curse as the man disappeared into the trees.

Killian turned around.

Mailin was trailing after him, trying to catch up. From his vantage point, he saw the beach, the bodies, and her diminutive frame.

With a sigh, he abandoned his chase.

It might be a mistake allowing a witness to live, but he wouldn't risk leaving her. The two newcomers had solidified his suspicion. The island teemed with prisoners who had not seen a woman in a long time.

NINE

MAILIN

The water flowed in a brackish slurry of sediment and sludge. It was so discolored, Mailin could barely see the pebbled bottom of the shallow stream. She frowned. Never had she seen fresh water the color of tea.

"How is the water brown?" she asked with a heavy sigh. "Guess we can't drink from it." She leaned against the closest tree and braced trembling arms on her thighs. Goddess of light, she needed food to fuel herself before she passed out.

Scar placed a steadying hand on her arm. He stood so close that the breadth of his shoulders blotted out the dappled light from the trees and shrouded her in his shadow.

"Here," he said, thrusting the waterskin at her.

Mailin cast chary eyes at his offering. "I already drank. You said we needed to pace ourselves."

He shrugged. "You need it. Take another mouthful."

As she took a grateful gulp, he murmured, "I'm sorry, but we can't stop for long. We must keep moving."

She swiped the sleeve of her shirt—his shirt—over her perspiration-beaded forehead and narrowed her eyes. "We must be halfway through this godsforsaken island by now." She was no longer nauseated by her boots, pilfered from the smallest corpse, ill-fitting though they might be. At least they kept her soles protected.

"We don't know how many prisoners reside here, or where." He gestured at the ground, bearing imprints of their tracks. "The soil is too loamy. If someone tried to track us, they could easily find us."

Knots twisted in her belly, but she no longer knew if they were from fear or hunger. "You covered our tracks back there," she pointed out. The bondsman had painstakingly erased their footsteps across the sandy beach with a leafy branch. When they'd trekked through the dense forest, he had taken more time to cover their tracks across the silty soil. He'd only stopped doing that when he deemed them deep enough into the woods. Mailin couldn't imagine anyone tracking them here.

"I've obscured our prints, but I can't erase all evidence of our presence. A real tracker can easily find us." His gaze was sharp, and an undercurrent of urgency laced his tone. He scanned their surroundings for the fifth time since they'd paused, though it had been less than two minutes.

Mailin reached into the pocket of her stolen breeches and palmed the shorn fabric she'd slipped in there, seeking comfort as she usually did by fingering the embroidery. "We don't know if anyone is looking for us," she protested. "Shouldn't we stick to the coastline and hope for a passing ship?"

Scar shot her an incredulous look. "We would be easy prey if we stayed out in the open. It is unlikely ships would sail close enough to the Isle of Groydon to spot us. Even if they did, they wouldn't pay us any heed." He shook his head. "We must find a place to hide until we find a way to return to Amereen." He surveyed their surroundings once more before extending his hand. "Come along, my lady."

Despite all her discomfort, she found the strength to scowl. "Why do you insist on calling me that? I told you my name is Mailin."

Her outburst only earned her a frown. "You are my lord's betrothed. That makes you my lady."

"Betrothed, not wife."

Hearing him acknowledge her betrothal made her cringe inwardly. Perhaps it was her uncanny attraction to him, this enigmatic bondsman with his scarred face and disarming smile, or perhaps it was because the title honored her with unfounded respect. Mailin might be a lady born, but she was not a lady bred.

She was little more than a liar and a cheat.

"And after what I just did?" She gave a weak laugh. "He's probably happy to see me rot here."

"Vale can be"—he expelled a breath—"wicked at times, my lady, but he's not entirely heartless." He shifted on his feet. "He tried to pull your dinghy back toward the ship, but the storm had carried you too far from his reach."

"Well, he shouldn't have sent you after me," she mumbled, even though she inwardly thanked Railea he had. "You could have drowned."

Scar stooped so his head came closer to her height, and his gaze held hers with such intensity, she could not look away. "Know this, my lady. Vale did not send me. I jumped in after you because there was no other way."

Her heart skipped, but her lips pinched. "Fool. If you had left me to my fate, then you wouldn't be in this mess."

A furrow appeared between his brows. "Your life is worth a hundred of mine."

Mailin frowned back at him. She had spent all her life scrap-healing for the poor, and if there was one thing she'd never questioned, it was the immeasurable worth of life—*all* life. "You can't possibly believe that."

"Of course I do."

"That's absurd. Even the goddess herself doesn't value life that way."

One side of his lips quirked in a half smile, lifting his scar and lighting his face in a way that made her heart rollick in her chest.

"I don't need Railea's judgment to see true value for myself. You have the power to save a life, while my worth lies in how quickly I can end one."

Killian snapped his mouth shut. He should not have expressed himself so, and her blinking eyes showed he had unsettled her.

"Come," he said abruptly. "We shouldn't waste time." They needed to find drinkable water, a way off this island, and—he shot his companion a worried look—some food. The pallor of her skin had turned sallow. The little gulps of water he allowed himself did little to stave off his own thirst.

"Scar?"

He grunted a nonverbal response as he mapped the land with his mind. Considering their trajectory from the shore and the increasing incline of their path, they were clearly moving to higher ground. Could they find a way to cross to the northeastern shore, the closest to Amereen's harbors? He hadn't expected such mountainous terrain, or polluted water. Then again, he could have guessed. He'd heard enough rumors to suspect the Isle of Groydon served as more than an open prison. Now he knew it to be truth. Declan Thorne, now the archmage of Amereen, was as shrewd as he was just. The knowledge brought a grim smile to Killian's lips. Even as a boy, Declan had always been cold.

"Scar?" Mailin repeated, her voice bringing him back to the present.

"Yes, my lady?"

Her nose wrinkled, likely from his stubborn use of formalities. It served as a good reminder for *him* of the clear rift between them.

"What's your name?"

He halted in his tracks, and she walked right into him, bumping into his back with a tiny *"Oof."*

Killian jumped forward and muttered an apology, but her query hung between them, as patent as the humidity of the air.

"You already know." he quickened his pace, wishing he could escape the question with simple haste.

A scowl filled her tone. "Your real name."

"Scar *is* my name."

When he offered no further explanation, she quipped, "How could that be? Surely you haven't always been . . ."

"Scarred?" He threw her an easy smile, but he couldn't completely censor the bitterness in his tone. "No, I wasn't born this way, but Scar is what I've been called for as long as I can remember." A blatant lie.

Once, he'd had a real name. Once, he'd been a cherished son. But that boy was no longer, and there was no sense reopening old wounds.

She stared at him. The tiny furrow between her brows suggested skepticism, but thankfully, she didn't press further.

They had barely taken three steps before she asked, "How old are you? You can't possibly be much older than Vale . . . Have you worked for him your whole life?"

He frowned even as a small thrill coursed through him. Not only did she care to learn his name, but she also seemed genuinely interested in *him*—a man often ignored. People preferred not to see his scars, so they pretended not to see him at all.

"I'm sorry," she added quickly. "Ignore me. I didn't mean to pry." She trudged a little farther before pursing her lips. "Actually, I take it back. I did mean to pry."

Killian raised his brows and received a wry smile in return.

"I'm just curious," she said, "and I need to talk before I lose my mind thinking of the man I just murdered" —a grim shake of her head—"or the fact that we're stranded on an island meant to imprison bloodthirsty criminals."

"He deserved to die. All of them did." Killian was unable to keep the edge from his voice at the thought of what Eyeball Paddy and his friends would have done to her had she been at their mercy. "They were dead the moment they decided to hurt you."

An odd sheen colored her eyes before she pulled her gaze away. They took a few more steps in silence before Killian, hating the sudden awkwardness, wracked his brain for something to fill the quiet.

"I'll turn five hundred and thirty-three this summer," he muttered when he remembered her question.

Her head lifted. "You're older than I thought. And you've worked for Vale your whole life?"

Killian responded with a grunt because it was yet another question he didn't want to answer. She parted her lips, but Killian stopped her next query with a shake of his head. There were too many things about his past he preferred not to say.

"If you tell me something about yourself . . . ," he said, because he enjoyed listening to her voice more than he cared to admit. "I'll tell you something about me. How about that?"

The curve on her lips sent another thrill through him.

"Sounds fair. What would you like to know about me?"

Everything. Instead, he shrugged. "Have you always had a

predilection for jumping off ships in the middle of a storm?"

Her smile deepened as she mimicked his nonchalant shrug. "I'll admit, I am prone to recklessness. My father called me the devil's spawn so often that I decided to make good on it." An impish smirk. "Once, I managed to evade my parents to scale the tallest tree I could find in the manor grounds." Her smile faded. "Just before I reached the top, I lost my footing. Not only did I end up with a twisted ankle, but Father broke it for good measure."

Her words were spoken with such indifference, his breath hitched as he halted to stare at her. "He broke your ankle? For falling out of a tree?"

She shrugged as though it were a common enough occurrence. "He did it because I defied him. He wanted it to serve as a reminder, so I'd never climb trees again. It was unladylike, he said."

Killian clenched his fists.

"My turn," she said with a distracting grin. "So, have you always been inclined to jump off ships in the middle of a storm after wayward damsels?"

The edges of his lips twitched.

"I'll admit, I've always had a secret wish of getting hit on the head by a paddle," he said with exaggerated somberness.

She burst into a giggle before clamping hands over her mouth to stifle the sound. Sensible. They didn't want to draw unwanted attention. Yet he was already eager to hear more of her unfettered laughter.

She shot him an expectant smile, and he realized she was waiting for his next question. Delight warmed beneath his ribcage, however absurd it might be given their current predicament. "Why were you climbing the tree in the first place?" He couldn't shake the image of her—a child, prim and proper—climbing a tree.

"I was just trying to see beyond the walls. I wasn't allowed out much, and that only made me want it more."

He frowned. He recognized the yearning in her voice. He, too, had never been afforded the freedom to roam as a child, not since the moment he'd been confined to the enclave.

Her hand slipped into her pocket and drew out a strip of red cloth, which she twirled absently around her fingers.

"What's that?"

She gave a sheepish smile. "I tore it from the hem of my grenadi."

At his befuddled expression, she showed him the scrap of fabric embroidered with a bird. A swan, with its wings stretched in flight. "The dress was one of my favorites because of this. I couldn't bear to leave it behind." She stroked the stitched wings with the reverence of an acolyte before Railea's altar.

"What makes it so special?" he asked. The embroidery appeared timeworn, its threads almost tattered.

"The swan is from a lullaby Mamma used to sing."

Killian cocked his head. "A lullaby?"

"You asked me two extra questions," she protested, clearly eager to change the subject. "It's my turn."

He acquiesced with a nod.

She continued to toy with the little scrap while he tried to not stare at the leather clinging to the flare of her hips.

"Where would you go"—her gaze flicked to his collar for the briefest instant before returning to his face—"if you had the chance?" If he was free.

Killian looked down at his boots. His indenture had never been in question, so he had never indulged himself with wishes and wants. He'd learned long ago not to dwell on such things. Dreams were for men free to make their own choices, not for the likes of him.

Mailin peered up at him with expectant eyes, as though she

truly cared to learn of his long-stifled aspirations. He found himself speaking words he hadn't in centuries. "I would find someplace quiet and peaceful, somewhere remote. Perhaps a small village far from the capital where I could tend to the land and grow my own crops."

He would build his own home, a small cottage with a cozy hearth, just large enough for him and perhaps, if he was lucky, a woman who could overlook his scars long enough to warm his bed on occasion. He didn't say the latter aloud, of course. A lady wouldn't understand or appreciate his baser desires.

"A farmer." She raised her brows at him. "I would never have guessed." The wondering smile dancing across her lips rendered her so achingly beautiful, Killian stumbled over a patch of tangled weeds. He righted himself before she could reach for him and cleared his throat to mask his embarrassment. "In a different life, perhaps."

"Perhaps," she said with a wistful sigh.

"And you?"

"If I had the chance, I'd be a nomad." A glimmer of excitement lit her tone. "I'd trade scrap-healing for coin. Travel from one province to the next. I'd see the mountain ranges of Amereen, hike the golden sand dunes of Teti Unas, and make my way all the way up north, to the fabled glaciers of Flen. I want to see it all." She chuckled and absently waved the little scrap of fabric in her hand like a child clutching her special blanket. "Well, at least now I can say I've seen the unsavory Prison Island firsthand."

Not for the first time since he'd donned his silver collar of servitude, Killian yearned to be rid of it. Now the yearning turned almost desperate. His stride slowed as something else occurred to him.

"Scrap-healing," he mused and lifted a low-hanging bough so she could pass. "Is that what you were doing when . . ." He cleared his throat. "In the alleyway?"

She scuffled past him with her head dipped, and he wondered if she remembered their first meeting as keenly as he did. "Yes, though I was there that night for more selfish reasons. There was someone I knew there that I had hoped to sway to come with me." She shook her head. "Now I'm glad she didn't."

"With your station and your skills, you could have lived your dreams, my lady. Why agree to marry Vale? The wife of a high mage will rarely be afforded a chance to travel."

She wrinkled her nose at him as though the reason should have been obvious. "Marrying a foreign dignitary like Vale is the only way I can leave home on my own terms." She shuddered. "If it were up to my father, he would have sent me to the Keep, and I can't think of anything more damning than being an archmage's . . . bedmate."

In truth, Killian could think of several fates more wretched, yet anger slid its scalding fingers beneath his breastbone all the same. A creature as glorious as her should be free to live her life, not confined to the bed of some archmage who owned so many ayaris that she would likely be nothing more than a faceless body. Then he frowned. "Was it not your father who wrote to Vale to set up the betrothal?"

Mailin's cheeks pinkened to match the tiny freesias freckling the ground. She tucked the scrap of fabric back into the pocket of her breeches and fidgeted with a strand of hair falling over face. "Father would never have reached out to a lord in Amereen."

Killian's mouth parted when realization dawned. He could only stare, baffled by the beguiling blend of blushing cheeks and brazen will. Suddenly, it no longer seemed egregious that she'd jumped off a ship in the height of a storm. A woman audacious enough to lure a high mage into an engagement contract seemed precisely like the reckless sort who had no qualms tempting fate.

Or him, for that matter. He swallowed as he continued to stare at her, unable to wrench his gaze away.

They were not so different after all. Her dreams were as unattainable as his own, and somehow, that stung him more than his own abandoned wants. Compared to the verve and vim of her dreams, his own aspirations were prosaic and pale.

She was a restless soul. A little reckless, a little rash, but filled with vivacity bright enough to blot out the sun. Killian wanted her to see the brilliance of the starlit skies from Amereen's rugged coastline. He wanted to *see* her skip through the frigid riverbanks of Flen lit only by the shine of the moon, and dance upon the rolling dunes of Teti Unas beneath the glorious flare of the setting sun.

He wanted to place the world at her fingertips, yet he was nothing but a helpless bondsman with nothing to give. Still, Killian grabbed the crook of her arm, needing to offer the one small thing he could—reassurance.

"My lady," he murmured. "Vale can be . . ." Killian wracked his brain for an unoffending word. "*Temperamental*," he grated between clenched teeth, "but he is not wicked." He truly believed that. Vale might be deviant in his sexual habits, but he was not usually iniquitous . . . except with Killian, of course. When it came to Killian, Vale derived a perverse satisfaction in debasing him whenever he could.

Her lips flattened to a seam.

Killian sighed. "One day, he'll learn to treat you the way you deserve." How could Vale *not*? Any man fortunate enough to call her his had to see beyond her beauty and her bloodline to the stunning rarity of her spirit.

Silence weighed heavy between them, and Killian shuffled his feet, suddenly shamed. He hadn't offered her reassurance; he had merely spoken words to comfort *himself*. He knew better than anyone of Vale's tendencies toward rexweed and liquor, a disturbing combination that hardened a man's fists and heightened his taste for violence.

Still, Killian had hoped a wife would afford Vale the motivation to stem his addictions. Without the influence of those substances, Vale was capable of gentleness. Killian had witnessed it before.

He clenched his jaw so hard, an ache formed at his temple. Barely a week of betrothal, and Vale had mistreated her aboard the ship, free from the influence of his vices. Had Vale always been such a brute, and Killian willfully ignorant?

A more troubling notion had his hands in fists. What if his hopes were unfounded, and Vale continued to mistreat her long after marriage? Would Killian stand idly by, watching bruises decorate Mailin's skin? He could hardly stand it when Vale mistreated his whores and paramours—all who had gone willingly to his bed. But Mailin?

Bile rose in his throat at the thought of her in Vale's bed. For the first time in his life, he envisioned his hands around Vale's neck, throttling the lord alive.

Mailin released a derisive laugh, disrupting his dark thoughts. "For Vale to treat me the way I deserve . . . Like a common whore, you mean?"

Killian flinched. Her choice of words reminded him of his own trespasses when they first met.

"I am sorry." He rubbed the back of his neck, which grew more heated with every breath. "The first time we met, I should never have assumed . . . I'm sorry."

Amusement glinted in her eyes. "I can hardly blame you. The alley of Madam Sima's isn't exactly a place you'd expect a lady to be, is it?"

Killian knotted his brows as the heat from his neck climbed to his cheeks. "My behavior was inexcusable."

Her lips twitched.

Killian was so enthralled by the peek of her pearlescent teeth between her pink lips that he nearly missed the snap of a distant twig, closely followed by muted laughter. Without another word, he yanked Mailin to her knees and dragged her behind a riotous shrub.

He placed a finger over her lips, and she nodded, her eyes wide with understanding. Still crouching, Killian shuffled to peer beyond the path.

Sickness oiled his gut.

They'd inadvertently walked straight to the prisoners' camp.

TEN

MAILIN

Mailin leaned against Scar, squinting to see past the considerable breadth of his shoulders. A settlement lay ahead. A banked pyre of soot dominated the center, surrounded by crudely built tents fashioned from wide, fanlike leaves, vines, and scraps of indeterminate animal hide. Her brows drew together as she noted the large, wooden chests at the periphery of the camp, filled with what appeared to be lumps of granite.

Two men labored over an antiquated well surrounded by river stones. One man was so heavily tattooed his forearms appeared to be a canvas of dark swirling lines, while the other had ginger hair and blotchy, sunburned skin. Both wore pickaxes strapped at their backs.

Excitement rose in her chest. "They have a *water well*," she said on a low hiss, meant only for Scar's ears. Awareness of her own hunger and thirst renewed as she eyed the men drinking from the bucket.

Scar gave her a soft grunt of acknowledgement, his head

turning the direction of a third man who strode into view. The newcomer, a rather stocky man, carried a bucketful of—*rock?*—toward the wooden chests and added to the contents.

One of the men by the well called out, "Working hard there, eh, Drey?"

The stocky newcomer, Drey, scowled at the two loitering by the well. "As you should. Lord Commander's to arrive any day now."

Mailin's heart pounded in her ears.

"Save yerself the trouble, ye dumb sod," replied the tattooed man with a snort. "The warden will take whatever the lord commander brings. Leave nothing but scraps for us."

Drey scrubbed his dirt-stained face with the sleeve of his shirt. "Warden left new shoes for us the last time, di'n' he? And the hides? If it's scraps he's offerin', I'll take 'em. 'Sides, maybe this time the Lord Commander will bring meat again."

The one with the sunburned skin smirked, showcasing darkened spots where teeth should be. "Haven't you heard? We've fresh meat tonight"—a hair-raising chortle—"Paddy and his lot, lyin' in the sand like driftwood, Yorn said. The bastards likely taste foul, but Finneous will carve up the best bits. Freshly slain, too. No sense lettin' good meat go to waste, eh?"

Drey sauntered closer to the well and grabbed for the water bucket. "Eyeball Paddy and his band of brothers?" No surprise in his voice, as though death were a standard occurrence. "Who did the honors?"

"Yorn swears they were done in by some scary bonecracker with a maimed face aaand . . . ," —the sunburned man as he waited for Drey's full attention— "A woman! A proper one, with tits almost spilling out of her dress."

Mailin slapped a hand over her mouth to stifle her gasp. Beside her, Scar stiffened visibly, his muscles taut and motionless, like a snake liable to strike at the slightest provocation.

"A woman? *Here*?" Drey asked, disbelief high in his tone. Water dripped off his scruffy, black beard to dribble on his shirt.

The tattooed man gave a dismissive huff. "Bah! Yorn's probably addled by mind maggots, if ye ask me. Fuckin' archmage wouldn't be so kind as to indulge us with cunt."

"At least we won't need to fight to feast tonight!" said his comrade. The resulting cheer of agreement from the other two drew chill bumps down the length of Mailin's arms and roused nausea in her stomach.

She buried her face in Killian's side and shuddered. He didn't move away. In fact, he edged closer, cupping a gentle hand over the back of her head as though to comfort her.

When the men moved from hearing distance, Mailin released a huff of disbelief. "They're *eating* the corpses?"

Scar grimaced. "While we've been in the woods, I've been watching for signs of game. I haven't seen any animal tracks . . . and these men have likely been here a long time."

So long, it appeared every shred of civility had been stripped.

Mailin couldn't bring herself to comprehend. "This is an *island*. They could fish . . . or something."

"I doubt the men could venture from the shore enough to fish for anything more substantial than what washes up on the beach. The wards likely keep them confined."

"That's . . . cruel." To keep the prisoners on an island, yet bar them from taking sustenance from the sea . . . An unfathomable sentence.

Scar only shrugged. "Archmages are not known for compassion."

Mailin swallowed, trying to push past the knot in her throat before glancing back at the camp. "What about what they said?

Some commander is coming."

Another grunt. "Best thing I've heard all day. Sounds like a warden *is* stationed here. We should find him. Maybe we should track these prisoners. Doubtless, they'll make their offering soon."

"Offering?"

Scar nodded at the large chests filled with rocks. "Gold ore."

Mailin's eyes widened. "Those lumps are *gold?*"

Amusement lit his eyes. "Don't you speak the old tongue?"

Father hadn't educated her in the old mage tongue. She had learned to read and speak the common tongue much on her own. Father always believed educating women was a waste—after all, in his eyes, she was nothing but a walking womb.

"Groydon is the Magerian word for *gold*. The prisoners haven't been sent here merely for incarceration. They are here to mine. To the death."

usk had fallen, and even through the darkening skies, Mailin could see the incredulity in Scar's stare.

"No," he said on a growl. "That is *not* an option."

Mailin sighed and shifted her legs, wincing at the tiny pinpricks needling her sleeping feet. "What else do you propose?"

They'd been hiding there, beneath the leafy shroud of the underbrush, biding their time. In those short hours, she'd learned two things about Scar. One, for all the roughness of his exterior, he was curiously shy. At first, he'd tried to ward off her attempts to heal the little cuts and grazes he'd acquired from his altercation at the beach, but once she finally wore him down, she'd noticed the color rising up from his neck to darken beneath his cheeks whenever her fingers touched his skin.

Two, he was more obstinate than an ox.

They'd been in accordance that their next best course of action was to track the men the next morning in hopes they'd lead to the warden. They'd also agreed to remain here, cloistered between boughs, bark and dense foliage as they waited for dusk . . . because they needed water.

The source of drinkable water was just paces away, well within sight, well within reach. The only problem was the men occasionally carting bucketfuls of gold ore.

"There is *no* one around right now. I could sneak into the camp and refill our waterskin," she said, dragging out the word *water* for emphasis. He must be as parched as she.

"*I* should be the one to go," he hissed. "What do you think they'll do to you if you get caught?"

Mailin sighed and held up a finger. "You're so large it'll be hard for you to sneak in and out quickly." She lifted a second finger. "You're also wearing a metal collar. If you run into someone, they're bound to notice it." A third finger. "You're also . . ." She bit down on her lips before she could say *wickedly distinctive* in reference to the scars on his face. She mumbled "recognizable" instead.

His gaze dropped to his feet and Mailin felt the sudden urge to kick herself. The taut silence lasted but a moment before he proved himself more stubborn than a herd of stampeding oxen.

"No one is ever going to mistake you for anything but a woman, my lady." He said in an obvious attempt to dissuade her from her plans. Unfortunately, he only reminded her of her station, her gender and, in combination, her inability.

Mailin narrowed her eyes. She responded by reaching for his belt buckle, her hand snaking around his trim waist. His eyes went round with such comical shock that Mailin had to bite her inner cheek to hold in the laughter tickling her throat. She had scrap-healed many men—some old, some young, and most were often so wrung out by poverty that they were all but skin and bones—but never a statuesque one like him.

Healthy, well-thewed men often wanted a woman for something baser than healing, and Mailin had no desire to put herself in such a position.

With *Scar*, however . . .

She edged so close that the little space between them crackled with heat that was more than the warmth exuded by their bodies. Despite the lingering sweat, blood, and death that clung to him, she scented brine, warm, male skin, and something so intoxicatingly virile that her tongue darted out unbidden to lick her lips. He held himself so motionless she couldn't even hear him breathe. His irises, a rich honey brown, were so dilated she saw herself reflected in them, bold and brazen. When her fingers delved under the hem of his shirt and brushed his skin, he jolted as though struck by a lightning bolt.

"What are you doing?" His voice grew husky, rousing more heat beneath her skin. Mailin smirked when she found what she was looking for—hard and smooth as stone.

She withdrew her hand and waved the knife triumphantly between them.

His brows furrowed.

Without further thought, Mailin gathered her thick mane and began sawing through it with the blade.

"What are you *doing?*" he repeated, this time as though accusing her of sacrilege. He made a grab for her forearm, but Mailin shrugged off his hold and pinned him with a glare.

"It's my hair." She continued to butcher it. She winced as the less-than-sharp blade tugged hairs straight from her scalp, but the knife was still serviceable. She let the severed ends fall to the ground and ran her fingers through the shortened strands that barely reached her shoulders. Satisfied with the length, she wound it up into a topknot the way some men did and secured it with her precious, embroidered scrap of fabric.

She dug her fingers into the dirt. Allowing herself a grimace, she smeared it liberally over her face, taking extra care to rub it over the side of her neck where the rune of revocation was typically seared. When she was satisfied with her handiwork, she grinned up at him. "Well?"

He did not appear impressed. In fact, he looked on the verge of a conniption with his lips pressed firmly together, his white scar stark against the red streaking his cheeks. He parted his lips, and Mailin braced herself for a stinging tirade, but it never came. He snapped his mouth shut, shifted in his seat as though gnats were crawling up his pants, then opened his mouth again.

Finally, he expelled a heavy breath. "No one," he said through gritted teeth, "is going to believe you're a man." His eyes dipped pointedly to her chest, then her hips until heat scored *her* cheeks.

Mailin huffed and untucked the hem of his shirt. "It's long enough to cover my hips, and I'll hunch my shoulders."

"Are you always this stubborn?"

Mailin gaped at the accusation. The nerve of the man. "I'm not stubborn; you are! I just want to get us some water."

"*I* can get us water."

She lifted her chin. "You may think I'm some pampered lady, but I assure you I am not. I never wait for someone else to do something I can do for myself."

He frowned, looking at a loss for words.

She shrugged. "Besides, if I do get caught, at least you'll be there to rescue me. The same cannot be said if *you* were to be caught."

"If I were caught, I'd expect you to keep your distance, find the warden, and escape." Flat, serious words. Stupid words. She would never run while the prisoners cannibalized him. Scar seemed to realize this, too, for his shoulders slumped as he released a resigned sigh.

He reached up to grip her chin, running his callused thumb over the edge of her jaw, and a sensual shiver slid down her spine. He rubbed a spot on the tip of her nose, his eyes filled with such tenderness that a strange ache formed in her ribcage.

"All right," he said after a long pause. "May Railea have mercy on anyone who catches you." He spoke with such dark malevolence that she beamed.

"I'll refill the waterskin and be right back," she said with the same sort of confidence she always felt when she set her mind to do something that would have had Leisa's brows rising. "They won't even notice I'm there."

The bucket hit the bottom of the well with a splash louder than a crack of thunder. Mailin cringed and glanced over her shoulder, certain someone must have heard her, but the camp remained silent and still.

She sucked in a breath. *Hurry, hurry, hurry!* She shot a quick glance at the thick foliage in the distance, finding reassurance in the weight of Scar's gaze even though she couldn't see him.

She grasped the wooden handle and began turning the well's pulley. A low, somber creak sounded before it began cranking, the bucket protesting in splishes and sploshes. The bucket was barely halfway up before the muscles of her arms began to quiver. *How could water feel so heavy?*

After what seemed an eternity, the wooden rim of the bucket came into view. Retrieving it from the center of the well was trickier than she expected. With a grunt, she leaned far over the curved edge of the well to reach for it.

A large hand slapped her shoulder.

Mailin jumped, and the bucket almost tipped right back into the well. She froze, her heart rising to her throat.

"Move aside, lad," grumbled a gruff voice at her back.

Swallowing hard, Mailin blanked her expression before turning around to a sneering man with an unkempt beard and a head so bald that moonlight glinted off the crown like shaved marble.

Mailin secured the waterskin over her shoulders before attempting what she hoped was a curt, manlike nod and backing away.

"Haven't seen ye around before," he said, narrowing his eyes.

Despite the dread coagulating like sludge in her throat, Mailin squared her shoulders. He reminded her vaguely of a sniffing dog. Darting off like a hare would probably entice him to chase.

She lifted her head with a haughty tilt of her chin, roughened her voice, and injected a drawl into her tone. "I'm new here." Scar had speculated that Prison Island was likely the size of a large town, accumulating several hundred denizens over the years.

Unlikely for one convict to have met *everyone.*

His gaze roamed over her person. "New, eh? Been enjoying the Dragon's Teeth, have ye?"

Mailin blinked. "Dragon's Teeth?"

"You fresh bloods move ore to the tower, don't ye?"

At the mention of the tower, Mailin's ears pricked. "I . . . ah, yes."

He pinned her with gimlet eyes, causing her throat to constrict. She mustered more confidence and said, "Sure I do. You been there? The Dragon's Teeth?"

"Been there?" He snorted. "Nearly died there! That there devil valley's claimed the lives of many bastards, each one meeting their end carting ore to that worm of a warden. And a little thing like ye . . ." He chortled. "Ye won't last long at the Teeth. If yer smart, you'll learn to suck the right cock and git yerself out of the Teeth and into the mines." He narrowed his eyes. "What did ye do to git yerself here, anyway?"

Mailin blinked. "I . . . killed a man."

The convict smirked. "Oh, haven't we all?" He tipped the bucket up and guzzled, water drenching his beard and tunic.

Mailin could have walked away then, but the need to find out more about the warden held her back. "The warden. He lives in the tower? Is he the one who decides who works where?"

He emitted a satisfied belch and wiped his mouth with his forearms. "Don't waste yer time with the warden. Lazy oaf does nothing but lounge in his tower, acting like he's the archmage hisself, he does. If you're looking for the right cock . . ." A slow smile displayed crooked teeth, raising the hairs at the back of Mailin's neck. "I can definitely shorten yer line to the mines."

Mailin blinked. Surely, he was not suggesting . . .

"I've tried many boys around here. None quite as small as ye."

Mailin curled her lips and made to move away. "Sod off! I don't need anything from you."

Before she knew it, he grabbed her, fast as a snake, and turned her so she was shoved against the stone rim of the well. "Who do ye think ye are?"

"Someone you're going to regret touching, that's who!"

He scoffed and pulled out a crude but sharp-looking dagger. It gleamed like ivory, though it was likely fashioned of bone.

"Got a tongue on ye, eh?" He brandished the blade. "We'll see how ye snap when I cut it right out of that pretty face of yers."

She tried to twist herself free, but he only shoved harder, pressing her flat against the rounded wall of the well. He clamped a hand at her chin, his fingers pushing against her cheeks to force her mouth open.

His fingers eased abruptly.

Mailin jerked her chin up to see Scar looming over them, fury etched in every line of his face as the convict slumped at his feet. A bloodied knife glinted in his hand.

"Scar," she cried, realizing her mistake the moment his name left her lips. When he glanced at her, distracted, the convict struck like a viper. The bone dagger proved to be sharp, cutting a gash through the fabric of Scar's tunic. From her bondsman's grunt of pain, she knew the attacker's aim had struck true.

Scar relieved the convict of his weapon with alarming force. He twisted the man's wrist backward. The dagger dropped to the ground, followed by a disturbing crack and the convict's yowl. In the next instant, the convict lay on his back, staring sightlessly up at the sky with his mouth agape and blood welling like a crimson sash across his throat.

Scar wiped his knife across the corpse's tunic.

"Railea's blood," Mailin stammered. "We need to run." Leaving the corpse would undoubtedly draw more attention. Given the conversation they had overheard previously, some of the prisoners were already aware of their presence.

When she looked up at Scar, her heart stuttered. His eyes were oddly dilated.

"Scar?" she whispered warily.

He stood hunched, a hand pressed against his gut where he'd been struck. She stumbled toward him, hands outstretched and ready to heal. But she didn't get a chance, for Scar lifted his head with an urgency that stopped her cold in her tracks, scanning the area like a fox scenting a pack of hounds.

Voices rose in the distance—more men emerging from the clearing. Mailin froze at the same time the group of prisoners did.

All conversation ceased for an instant before someone shouted, "What in the five flaming hells is going on?"

Scar gripped her wrist. *"Run."*

ELEVEN

KILLIAN

They barreled through the woods, weaving past dense thickets and gliding over gnarled roots, guided by stray slivers of moonlight shining through the canopy. The side of his abdomen stung, but they couldn't afford to slow. He kept a firm grip on Mailin's wrist, guiding her through the labyrinth of trees even though he heard no pursuers.

"Slow down," Mailin panted. "Scar, please."

He couldn't stop, his legs driven by a will of their own. He couldn't seem to let her go, either. His fingers refused to release her slender wrist. All he knew was the need to remove her from danger. The image of her shoved up against the well, squirming against the ill intentions of another man refused to abate, fueling the adrenaline in his blood.

Mailin stumbled, falling to the ground with a yelp that turned to a gasp as he lifted her straight off her feet to cradle her like a child. She certainly weighed like one.

He kept moving, his surroundings blurring in a haze of green and gloom. Dimly, he felt her arms encircling his shoulders, her fingers sliding beneath the fabric of his tunic. Tingling warmth bloomed where her fingers met his skin, spreading through his bloodstream like a slow, honeyed drug.

Even through the stifling effects of his collar designed to nullify his mageborn abilities, this time he *saw* her psychic presence as she brushed up against his mind and wrapped around it. She was a brilliant shimmer of color, shifting like northern lights dancing across the night skies, more resplendent than a rainbow after a storm.

He slowed, his chest heaving as he stared down into unblinking feline eyes.

"I think we've lost them." His voice hoarse to his own ears. "But we need to keep moving."

Strangely enough, she didn't demand to be released, nor did she retract her hands from his shirt as she continued channeling her healing energies into him. Instead, she gazed up at him with such open trust that something in his chest constricted.

"We should never have done that," he mumbled. "Water wasn't worth it. Why in the five realms did you even speak to him?" he asked, unable to keep his exasperation in check.

"I thought I could get him to talk about the warden." She told him about the valley called Dragon's Teeth and the Tower.

"We have no idea which direction to head, much less where to go to find a place called Dragon's Teeth." He bit out the words. "And now we've left one more body in our wake, and more of them have seen us."

She dipped her head, clearly chastened.

Killian sighed. "I'm sorry."

Her brows knitted. "You're right. I shouldn't have dallied."

He tightened his hold instinctively. "I shouldn't have let him close enough to even touch you."

A raindrop fell on her cheek, smearing the dirt on her face. Another droplet followed. And another.

"Oh, *wonderful*." Mailin glared up at the drizzling sky with her nose wrinkled. "Must the gods torment us so?"

It was as though even the skies couldn't resist her, reaching down to rain celestial kisses upon her cheeks.

Gods help him, for he couldn't help himself.

With the arm he had tucked under her back, he ran an errant knuckle across her cheek under the guise of wiping smudges from her face. She didn't cringe from his touch, so he allowed himself another self-indulgent stroke against her jawline before he pulled away.

A gust was already picking up, rustling the leaves and echoing through the woods as the drizzle intensified into a light rain. The isle was far south of Amereen, and the temperature could drop without warning. He needed to find shelter, or they might be spending the night in the cold and wet.

"Rain isn't a bad thing, my lady," he said, forcing himself to use her title. With her in his arms, that was the only reminder he had of the league between them. "It will only distort our tracks, and hopefully discourage the men should they attempt to hunt us. Buy us more time."

She pursed her lips. "I suppose you're right," she muttered before glancing up at the skies with a grudging sigh. She tilted her chin heavenward, parting her lips as though to drink straight from the sky. Not a bad idea, only the rain wasn't heavy enough for her to catch more than a few droplets to wet her tongue. Still, she made a show of licking her lips and shot him an impish smile. "You ought to try it. Take advantage of Railea's generosity."

Killian found it in himself to laugh.

She grinned up at him, and despite his weariness, her presence filled him with vibrance. It didn't matter that they were stranded on an island filled with the most depraved souls of Amereen. In this moment, Killian wouldn't wish to be anywhere but here, nor anyone but himself —the man fortunate enough to hold such a jewel in his arms, even if she could never belong to him.

He tightened his arms around her as he walked, memorizing the feel of her soft curves against his chest as rain enveloped them in a pitter-pattering cocoon.

He didn't get to enjoy the moment for long before the winds gusted and rain began falling in earnest, transforming gentle droplets to a stinging deluge that spurred his steps. Shelter. They needed to find a rocky outcropping, or even a tightly knitted grove of trees. Anything to get Mailin out of the storm.

Her grip around his shoulders tightened. "What's *that?*"

Through the weeping skies, Killian spied the clearing ahead. At first glance, it appeared as though an enormous gopher had plowed through the area, forming mounds of dug-up dirt in its wake. A mine. Carved into the rock face like an ominous black hole leading deep into the earth. Deserted makeshift workbenches, scattered buckets, and tools strewn on the ground gave it an added air of eeriness.

"If the gateway to the five hells exist, I'm sure that's it," he said with a wry smile.

"Then why are you walking toward it?" The alarm in her tone told him she did not appreciate his attempt at humor.

"What better place than to hide in plain sight?" The place appeared deserted. It was the perfect temporary shelter, though he didn't take another step forward while she appraised the mine with dubious eyes. The wind howled, and her shoulders sagged.

"Gateway to the five hells," she mused, wiping the rain trickling down her face. "Well, that seems a fitting place for shelter in this godsforsaken place, doesn't it?"

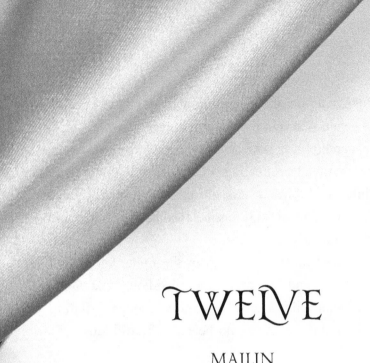

TWELVE

MAILIN

"We really shouldn't be here," Mailin whispered, as though they were in a place of pious worship and not a dank and deserted shaft mine. Scar had set her down on her feet, and she was ready to be back in his arms. The lichen covering the ground squished beneath her boots, and the air felt too cold. Healing Scar had robbed her of some of her energy, which caused her limbs to quiver but at the very least, they were out of the deluge. Her gaze darted from the rough-hewn walls down the pitch-black of the tunnel stretching deep into the earth. A crypt for the damned.

An uncontrollable shudder wracked her frame.

"The amount of vegetation growing at the entrance suggests this mine is long exhausted. Or perhaps I'm wrong, and the prisoners will be back at first light." Scar gave her arm a reassuring squeeze. "Either way, we'll be out of here as soon as the rain stops, but right now . . ." He removed the waterskin still draped over her shoulder, a wry smile on his lips. "It's my turn to take advantage of

Railea's generosity. You stay here."

Without giving her a chance to protest, he darted back into the torrent and headed straight for a nearby shrub with wide, tapered leaves. The waterskin was shaped like a bladder with a small, corked opening that made collecting water near impossible without a funnel. While Scar busied himself collecting raindrops that trickled from the tip of a leaf, Mailin squelched her instinct to follow and cling to him like moss on a rock.

So she stayed rooted at the lip of the mine, keeping Scar within her sights, and ignored the insidious clawing of claustrophobia. Thankfully, Scar returned soon enough, grinning as he shook the waterskin so she could hear the fruitful slosh of his efforts.

After they both drank, he repeated the process to refill the waterskin, and by the time he was done, he was well and truly drenched. His boots squelched, and water ran off him in tiny trickles as they ventured into the yawning tunnel that stretched into sepulchral darkness.

Never had she trusted a man so explicitly that she would willingly follow him anywhere. Even, she mused, through the gates of hell.

As soon as the thought crossed her mind, her heart pinched, forming a dull ache beneath her breastbone. *Fool.* The moment they left this wretched place, she had to escape him.

She couldn't forget that Scar was a bondsman in Vale's service.

He might protect her against the criminals on this island, but she couldn't allow herself to assume he would protect her against Vale.

Even if he could, she couldn't—wouldn't—place him in that position. As high mage, Vale was a lord of the realm. He could easily have a bondsman executed under the claim of disloyalty. The thought of Scar's death was so abhorrent, she ground her teeth until her jaw ached. The best thing was for her to carry out her plan. To disappear, through the Curator's service, so Vale could never find her. Yet the thought of never seeing Scar again carved a tunnel-sized hole in her heart, and suddenly the prospect of her long-awaited freedom appeared bleak.

Scar stopped. "We shouldn't go any further. We are deep enough to be shielded from the rain. Any deeper and I fear we'll lose the moonlight."

Relieved, Mailin nodded her agreement, painfully aware they were standing hand in hand in a dark and empty tunnel. He must have realized it at the same time, for he released her hand abruptly. He sat down with a resigned sigh, and squeezed water from the hem of his tunic.

Following his lead, Mailin sank to her haunches and leaned against the crudely carved wall. She was partially soaked, and her damp clothing drew a chill. She couldn't imagine how terribly uncomfortable it must be for Scar, who was thoroughly drenched.

"Do you want to . . ." She winced as her voice bounced down the eerie shaft. She dropped her voice to a whisper. "Take off your clothes to better wring them dry?"

His buckskin pants were sodden, too, and heat crawled up her cheeks at the thought of him removing them right beside her, so she quickly added, "I'll turn around."

"No, I'll be fine." But he did remove his boots.

An awkward silence descended as he fastidiously squeezed the dripping ends of his shirt and pants. She tried not to stare down the black depths or listen to the eerie whistle of the wind filtering through the tunnel. Though she knew it to be a mine, it felt more like a tomb.

"What if they find us in here? We'll be trapped," she whispered.

Though she could only see the silhouette of his profile, she knew he smiled.

"If they are actively hunting us, we'll be far easier to track in the open than in here," he murmured, his voice a soothing rumble. "We'll stay until the rain eases, then we'll make our way toward the northwest border. Find the warden. Convince him to return us to civilization."

His conviction chased away some of her despair but also deepened her despondency. The moment they left this island, she would have to leave him.

In the meantime . . . She scooted closer. "Show me your wound."

He paused before he said, "You healed it. Doesn't hurt anymore."

"Show me," she insisted. Though she'd already channeled healing energy into him while he held her and ran through the woods, she couldn't be sure if he was fully healed. Not when she couldn't see or touch the wound.

When he didn't protest, she drew the side of his soggy shirt up to uncover the laceration. A hiss escaped her lips. The dim light illuminated the gash and the dried blood around his skin. The convict had scored him deeper than she'd realized. At least it was no longer bleeding.

His breath hitched when she pressed her palm over his wound, his body tensing as though he couldn't stand her touch. Mailin ignored him. Flesh wounds were often inconsequential to mages—their bodies recovered far faster than humans'—but that didn't mean they felt no pain or were invulnerable to diseases.

As she coaxed healing energies into him, awareness caught up with her. Every act of healing drew her closer to the psyche of her patient, but Mailin always kept a firm distance on the psychic plane. Given the sort of people she scrap-healed in Jirin, she had no desire to glimpse their mind or form any sort of connection beyond healing. But this was *Scar*—the man who made her feel things no other ever had.

His psyche glowed with the brilliance of a burning star, beckoning her like a wayfarer's beacon. She slunk close enough that the vibrance of his mind warmed the edges of her own, and only then did she notice it. The brutality that marked his psyche echoed the scars on his skin. Fissures of black flowed like deadened rivers across the starlit brightness of his mind . . . but the effect only made him *more*. More intricate, more complex, more stunning. It was like watching a lightning storm unfurl across midnight skies in all its savage glory.

She drew close on the mental plane, helpless as a moth drawn to flame, until she rubbed her mind against his, inadvertently giving him a telepathic kiss.

He went motionless beside her.

Mailin withdrew—psychically and physically—with a gasp. "I'm sorry," she whispered. At least the darkness shrouding them hid the furious heating of her cheeks.

An awkward silence filled the air between them until he murmured, "I didn't mind it."

Mailin lifted her chin. Though the moon barely breached the tunnel, it seemed every sliver of light sought to tease the edges of his profile and highlight the angles of his face. He faced her where the light illuminated only the part of him untouched by violence, leaving the scarred side in the dark. In this angle, he was undeniably attractive even with his unkempt hair and scruffy beard. Handsome, in a rough and rugged kind of way.

Yet she itched to turn his face so she could see his scarred side.

To her healer's eyes, his scar was shocking and savage and brutal—yet strangely beautiful. It was silent evidence of a survivor's tale. A survivor who possessed a wild beauty that was the tempest of the sea before it swallowed her whole.

Her fingers found his face in the darkness and traced the jagged lines carved in his cheek. He drew in an audible breath and jerked away, as though her touch pained him.

"I'm sorry," she whispered again. "I didn't mean to . . ."

"Don't be. No one means to." Though his posture remained still as stone, he radiated pain that made her heart twist.

"You misunderstood me," she protested.

He gave a self-deprecating laugh. "You've already given me much grace, my lady. My scars are usually all people see, or they don't see me at all."

The twisting of her heart turned to a knot, and she reached for him again.

He shrugged her off. "Please, don't. You don't owe me anything." He turned his head obstinately to the opposite direction, fully exposing the scarred side of his visage as though to make his point.

Mailin narrowed her eyes. "I'm sorry to have embarrassed you, but I'm not sorry for touching you."

His head tilted the barest fraction, as though he wanted to face her but held himself back. Mailin laid her hand on the crook of his arm, willing him to turn around. He didn't.

"You're wrong, you know," she said. "I owe you my life." Tension returned to his frame, turning his muscles rigid beneath her fingers. "But it wasn't gratitude I felt when I touched you."

Though he probably couldn't see her properly due to the darkness, his head snapped toward her as though in disbelief. With a gumption she didn't know she possessed, Mailin leaned forward and pressed a kiss to the cheek that was imperfectly perfect.

His unsteady breaths filled the silence.

"What . . ." His voice came out raspy. He swallowed. "What

did you feel?"

"Awe." The word popped from her mouth before she could think better of it. And because it made his lips part and his eyes blink so rapidly, she decided his shock was well worth her modesty. "Affection," she added, and pressed another kiss to his face, this one over his beard, closer to the tail end of the longest scar, just before it met the side of his lips. Without lifting her lips away from his skin, she murmured, *"Desire."*

She seemed to have lit a fuse, for he sparked to life. He turned and drew her close until she was almost in his lap. The furious pounding of his heart filled her ears.

Or perhaps it was her own.

She hadn't quite thought things through. There was a reason she shouldn't be doing this, but at the moment she couldn't quite remember it. Why shouldn't she drink him in? He was so close, filling the air with the heady scent of the sea, musk, and virile man.

The first time they'd met, in the alley, she'd wanted to run her hands over the side of his bearded jaw and learn his taste. Breaching the minuscule distance between their faces, Mailin pressed her lips over his. A shiver slid down his frame, sparking a thrill in her bones.

Stop, the logical part of her mind screamed. Yet she didn't. Couldn't. He was mead in her veins, delicious and intoxicating, suffusing every part of her senses with an inexplicable need. Never had she wanted a man so much she felt drunk.

You're only going to get your heart broken, warned the most rational part of her.

Gods, but hadn't she always been reckless?

She lifted a defiant hand to stroke his angular jawline, relishing in the softness of his beard against her skin. A deep rumble escaped his throat, and it was the sexiest sound she'd ever heard.

He kissed her back, his lips molding over hers in a way that fit perfectly, as though they had always been two parts of a whole. She wound her fingers into his hair and a breathy sigh escaped her lips as she reveled in the taste of him. Illicit. Forbidden. Utterly divine.

His kisses grew ravenous and his touch, voracious. His hands cupped the back of her head, his fingers winding into her hair as though he were a man lost at sea, and she, his lifeline. Then one of his large, callused hands stroked down her spine in a slow and sinful caress before delving under her shirt and exploring the length of her back. She gave a soft moan and pressed herself closer.

He responded with a low groan of his own as he delved deeper into her mouth. Their ragged breaths and mating tongues echoed through the tunnel like erotic whispers.

"Mailin." Her name was a groan on his lips, a reverent plea. "Gods, you taste so sweet."

He touched her as though she were sacred, tasted her as though she were the finest wine and to be savored. When he tugged the hem of her shirt over her head, she complied readily. She barely felt the rush of cold for he was all over her in the next breath, kissing her collarbone, running the tip of his nose along the hollow of her neck while his hands explored her breasts.

Needing to touch him in kind, she slipped her hand under his shirt. Her fingers grazed the rigged lines of his abdomen as well as the raised scars that decorated his skin.

He stiffened. Abruptly, he released her and pulled away, his breaths shallow.

"Scar . . . ?" she whispered. "What's wrong? I—"

He shifted away with a grimace. "*No.*" He spat the word as though she were a misbehaving dog. "Don't touch me . . . What we're doing, it . . . it isn't right."

The air was a cold sneer on her skin, his sudden rebuff a slap across her cheek. Tears pricked at the corners of her eyes, and with jerky movements, she dragged her shirt back on and wrapped her arms around herself. What had she been thinking? Behaving like an eager whore, she had practically thrown herself at him. She hated herself. More, she hated the tiny sob that leaked from her throat.

"I'm sorry." His arms folded around her without warning, and drew her back against his chest. "I'm sorry, Mailin."

"Let go." She twisted against his hold, but he refused to release her.

"I'm sorry," he said on a raspy whisper. "Forgive me, please . . . I shouldn't have said that. I shouldn't have touched you that way."

His words only incited more rage. She clawed at his forearms, struggling to free herself. "Then let me go!"

He didn't. He continued to hold her with a tenderness that made her heart ache. "You're not mine, temptress. Do you understand that? You're not mine to touch."

Exhausted, she slumped in his hold, her head sagging over his chest. "I won't marry him."

Silence reigned. The only sound in her ears was the furious beat of his heart.

"No," he murmured, surprising her with his agreement. "You deserve better."

Mailin stared up at him as he stroked the crown of her head with gentle hands, as though she were a child to be coddled. "When we're back in Amereen, I'll take you to the capital. The Traveling Wagons will take you to Batuhan. Vale has no reason to believe you survived the storm."

Mailin swallowed. She could hardly believe what she was hearing. "Will you . . . come with me?"

"Once you're away from Vale, you won't need my protection—"

"I'm not talking about protection. I'm asking you to come

with me." She licked her lips. "To be *with* me."

His fingers stilled in her hair. "You deserve better, Mailin."

Trapped on an island of bloodthirsty prisoners, ensconced in his arms in the darkness of this dank hollow, with the taste of him still fresh on her lips . . . Mailin couldn't remember a time she'd felt happier.

She told him as much.

He produced an exasperated sigh. "You deserve someone who can give you everything you need. Everything you want."

She glanced up at him, not bothering to conceal her open adoration. "I agree."

He clenched his jaw with such force she could hear his teeth grinding. "I am *not* that man, Mailin. I can't give you the life you deserve, not even if I'm free." A humorless laugh. "I'm no different from the prisoners on this island."

"How can you say that?" she snapped, straightening her spine. "You're a protector, not a murderer." She cupped his cheeks with both hands, her thumbs stroking the length of his jaw. "You're a bondsman, not a prisoner. How many more years of service do you owe before your bond is paid?"

When he only stared back at her with haunted eyes, Mailin added, "I'll help you. I'll scrap-heal, save every coin—"

"There is no bond." Bleakness permeated his tone. "I serve Vale because I owe him a debt that can never be repaid. I—" He dragged in several ragged breaths as though it pained him to speak. "Vale is my brother."

THIRTEEN

KILLIAN

Killian shifted so his back hit the jagged walls, drawing more distance between them. The mere mention of Vale soured his mouth. What had he been thinking? Once again, he hadn't been thinking at all when it came to Mailin.

His brother's betrothed.

Killian cast his sight to the ground, disgusted with himself.

"What are you saying?" Mailin's shock hung between them like a thick pall.

He swallowed the sickness in his throat. He hadn't spoken of his relationship with Vale to another soul. The only people who'd known the truth had been his parents' servants, and even they were gone now. Vale had dismissed every single one since Father's death. No one who currently worked for the high mage Vale Teranos knew the truth about Scar—but Killian didn't mind.

In fact, he preferred it that way. No one knew him, and no one knew the sins and shame he carried beneath his scars.

Until now.

Until a woman with dreams larger than her spirit had kissed him with such fervent desire and looked at him as though he were some kind of hero. Only he was no hero. He was a soul so wretched he deserved no name.

"I was the firstborn child of the high mage Hendrik Teranos and his elorin de ana, Priscilia." That was all he could manage before his throat constricted, and he reached up to finger the collar around his neck. He had worn it for so long the metal band felt safe. Comfortable, even.

She gave him an encouraging smile.

Killian licked his lips and nodded at no one in particular. "I was unnaturally gifted for a mage. I'd mastered both telekinesis and telepathy before I reached my hundredth year."

Mailin's eyes widened, and Killian shifted uncomfortably. Though mages were a psychic race, it was rare for one to wield two psychic gifts and almost unheard of for children to do so. She was understandably impressed, but instead of pride, he only felt shame.

He swallowed. "I could even warp."

Her already wide eyes rounded to saucers. "You . . . you're a teleporter?"

"Not truly," he hastened to explain. "Only for short distances. From one end of the room to the other, and only to places within my line of sight. But that was enough to make my father think I could attempt Arksana."

"Ascension?" Mailin winced as the word echoed around them. She lowered her tone and stuttered, "Why would he—" She swallowed, as though at a loss for words. "Why would he risk his son's life in exchange for power?"

Killian shook his head. "Not for power. Glory."

Mages who survived Arksana became archmages—beings so powerful they could well be gods in the flesh—but the survival rate was dismal. Hundreds upon hundreds of mages had attempted

Arksana, but the gods had allowed only eight archmages in existence at any given time.

"My father was a proud man, and his belief in my potential became an obsession. He convinced my mother that I would be better off trained by guardians at the enclave."

At Mailin's furrowed brow, he added, "The Thorne Enclave was a training ground for the gifted . . . among other things. Father believed the Guardians could make me a true teleporter, worthy for Arksana."

His father had been even more bent on preparing Killian for ascension after Vale's birth. While Killian's younger brother grew to be a formidable telekinetic, Vale had never mastered beyond the one psychic ability. As a result, Killian remained the apple of his father's eye. The sterling firstborn who could do no wrong.

"I was eager to please my father." Killian, too, had been filled with delusions of grandeur. His father's near-fanatical obsession had made him believe ascension *was* his destiny—until he discovered otherwise.

Killian shook his head with a derisive laugh. "His pride was poorly placed. Even with the guardian's judicious training, I simply could not warp beyond my immediate line of sight. I was not a true teleporter. So my guardians began employing . . . harsher methods."

Killian shut his eyes and drew a deep breath. Reliving the memories was akin to driving the guardians' heated blade across healed scars. "They thought if I was desperate enough, I could be forced to warp."

"Scar . . . ," Mailin whispered. The weight in her tone alone told him he needn't continue, but Killian was already back in the sparse compound of the enclave, his knees quaking on the flagstones drenched with his own blood. "They chained me up. At first they used the whip, but I passed out often, so they reverted to other torture devices." His hollow laugh echoed as he recalled the unforgettable agony of various bone-crushing and skin-flaying instruments that had been used on him. "I couldn't withstand much. The only thing I *could* endure without losing consciousness was the knife."

Over and over and over again, the guardians had driven the edge of the blade through his skin, before his cuts could heal. When his body became desensitized to the torture, they heated the blade or applied salt to his wounds. The guardians had cut so frequently, so brutally, that they had scarred a being who didn't scar easily.

"Why didn't you make them stop?" Mailin's voice sounded dry, as though her tongue were made of shredded paper.

"I tried. I cried. Begged." Killian lowered his head. He had even soiled himself in his desperation, but the guardians had paid him no heed. "The guardians were mages of old. They'd lived so long in isolation they saw nothing wrong with bloodying a boy for his own benefit."

"Your father," Mailin said, "why didn't *he* make them stop?"

"He didn't know," Killian retorted quickly. Defensively. Even though an eon had passed, he remained unwilling to believe his father had knowingly left him at the mercy of the guardians. He chose to believe his father'd had no knowledge of what had been done to him behind those walls.

"The guardians' methods did work." Another mirthless laugh worked up to his throat. "One day, I warped . . . I warped out of those chains, out of the enclave, and right back home." Where he had appeared on the hearth by his mother's feet, bleeding and bawling and beyond rational sense. His mother—his sweet, soft, and lovely mother had taken one look at him and fallen to her knees in anguish.

"Mother tried to hold me. Comfort me. Only, her touch caused me more pain . . . and I was trained to warp in pain."

So he did.

But Killian had never warped with a live person clinging to him. He'd had no idea he had to consciously envelop his psyche around any living flesh in contact with him or risk distorting it. There was a reason the process was called *warping* and was inherent only to mages with the strongest of minds.

"When I rematerialized, I found my mother's arms still wrapped around me, her cheek still pressed to the top of my head, but the rest of her . . ." Killian choked on his next words. "The rest of her was missing."

The parts of her body that hadn't been touching him—her torso, her legs—had remained by the hearth. Severed, as though a butcher had cleaved her in two.

Mailin's hands flew to her mouth, muffling her speech. "Goddess of mercy."

"She died instantly," he said. His only solace was that his mother had felt no pain. "My parents were promised. Mated. My father, her elorin de han, died shortly after." No mated partner survived the death of the other.

He had effectively murdered both his parents.

"I'm so sorry, Scar."

"So am I," Killian muttered with no small amount of bitterness coating his tongue. "So am I."

If only he'd defied his father. If only he hadn't warped home to his mother. If only he hadn't mastered warping at all . . . If only, if only, if only. But *if only* mattered naught in reality. And the reality was how he had grown from a boy gifted and full of promise to a man wretched and full of regret.

Mailin looked at him intently, her gaze contemplative. "Is this why you serve Vale as his bondsman? You're paying penance?"

Killian gave a mirthless smile. "I stay with Vale because he's the only kin I have left. I serve him because I owe him a debt I can never repay. I ruined our family, robbed him of his parents. No amount of coin can make up for what I've taken from him."

Mailin reached up and pressed her fingers against the collar. "But why wear this?"

"Vale was terrified of me. He saw what had happened to our mother and . . ." Killian shook his head. "The collar was the only way to guarantee I could never warp again. It was the only way he could stand to be around me." Killian shrugged. "I deserved it."

She stared at him, her eyes bleak pools in the dim light, her fingers rubbing the embroidered swan on the scrap of red. Somewhere during his confession, she had reached up to undo the fabric from her hair, as though she hadn't known what to do with her hands.

"I stayed because I was little more than a boy myself. I stayed because he was a child. My brother. Sometime over the years . . . I let myself forget who I really was. Vale calls me Scar, and I let him because that's what I am. A walking scar on our lives."

"You can't believe that." Her voice soft, her gaze fierce. "You can't truly believe that."

How could he not? "Recently I tried to walk away, but I just can't." Not when he felt responsible for Vale. It had been their mother's death that caused his brother's addiction. Vale first used rexweed to help him sleep, but as the years passed, the high mage's use of the drug had morphed into a vice. One that often manifested in violence.

Killian dipped his head, his fingers brushing at the uncomfortable metal collar that had grown comforting in its familiarity. "Vale's grown accustomed to how things are . . . and in a way, so have I." He drew consolation from the fact that he was kept close enough to intervene in the instances when his brother's judgment was distorted from the drug.

"Scar . . . ," she whispered.

"Killian," he offered. He hadn't uttered his own name for so many years the word was almost foreign on his tongue. "Killian Hendrik Teranos."

She repeated his name softly, smilingly, as though she'd been given a wonderful secret. "I like it."

So did he. He liked it so much he was already yearning to hear her sweet, husky voice say it again.

Instead, he bit down on his tongue and told her the truth. "I am not a man you want to be involved with, Mailin. I have nothing to my name. Nothing to offer but a history soaked with blood and pain."

She remained silent, seeming to weigh his words.

Good.

Killian shifted toward the opening of the tunnel so he didn't have to see her withdrawal. The rain was slowly coming to a halt, and fog rose from the warmth of the earth, dimming the moon and shrouding them in hazy darkness. She was so quiet he could almost imagine he was completely alone, as he always had been, as he always would be.

Then she whispered, "I'm no stranger to blood or pain."

He remained unmoving, staring out to the open, so Mailin dropped her gaze to the scrap of silk in her fingers. "My mother died before I saw my hundredth summer," she said, tracing the familiar stitches of the swan in the darkness. "She died from childbirth, bleeding out before my eyes. I was powerless to heal her."

He shifted around, a frown on his face. "You were a child. You cannot be blamed for her death."

She nodded with a rueful smile. At ninety summers, she had been no older than a human child of eight years. "Her death lies on my father's hands," she agreed. "But sometimes I can't help but wonder . . . or wish that I had been born a boy, then perhaps all of it could be avoided."

In Jachuana, all wealth and titles were passed through the male line. "But Mamma bore him only girls. I was the first of seven daughters."

The furrow between his brows deepened. "The first of seven . . . What happened to your sisters?"

"Sold." The word tasted like poison on her tongue.

She tucked a strand of hair behind her ear to tap at the slightly pointed tip that reflected the Seelie blood in her veins. "*This was what saved me. A physical indicator of my inheritance of my mother's gifts. My sisters were not so lucky. They were all born with rounded ears and exhibited no other inkling of any Seelie trait. Since Father didn't believe in raising 'worthless girls,' he bartered every child who showed no halfbreed abilities to his peers in exchange for some manner of favor or alliance."

Leisa was the only sister Mailin had ever known. And only because Leisa had been sold to a jade caste lord who lived near the An Jin residence. Mailin wasn't as fortunate with her other sisters. Somewhere in the realm, she had five more who were lost to her.

"My father was a monster . . . but *she* enabled him." Mailin bunched the embroidered swan in her hands until her knuckles whitened. She forced herself to loosen her grip, to forget her anger over her mother's inaction. She clung instead to happier memories—of her mamma's lullabies, her stories, and impromptu dances around the kitchen.

"I think Father only married her because of her ability to enhance his crop yield. But Mamma was too scared to leave him, too scared to do anything. She remained by his side, bound to him even though they were not truly mated. He never loved her enough to make her his elorin de ana." She sucked in a breath and gave a shaky laugh. " I don't think he is capable of loving anyone enough to bind his soul to theirs. And since she had Seelie blood, she was able to bear him heirs without the mating bond."

And how disappointed her father had been to find his firstborn child was not only female but lackluster compared to her mother. Killian's somber regard unlocked the vault that weighed like bricks over her chest.

"I haven't inherited the Seelie gift for botany," she admitted. "I can't do anything but heal."

Even then, she couldn't heal diseases and ailments—she could only knit broken flesh and open wounds. She might impress humans, or come in handy on a battlefield, but in an average life? For a race such as theirs, supernatural healing wasn't a lauded ability.

"So my father kept trying for another child. He attempted to impregnate my mamma, year after year, hoping to beget a gifted son. He would force her to drink tonics to help her conceive . . . then he would force himself on her." The latter came as a tremulous whisper as she recalled the one time she'd hidden inside her mother's wardrobe, spying between the wooden slats, hoping to understand why Mamma would sob each time Father visited her chambers. After that night, she never hid in a wardrobe again.

"By the time my seventh sister was born . . ." Mailin gave a bitter smile. "Mamma simply did not wish to witness the loss of yet another daughter. Or perhaps her body was too worn."

Mages gestated three years for every birth and rarely bore more than one child every century. Jiiyi An Jin had borne seven in little more than *half* a century, only to see six sold to buyers of questionable intent. Father hadn't taken the time to find his daughters well-meaning foster families. He'd sold them the way he sold his crop—to the highest bidder.

"Either way, she left me," Mailin said, detesting the

vulnerability in her tone. "The moment she passed, my father insisted I take over what she did for his fields. I tried, but I couldn't. When I failed year after year to enhance the yield of his crops, Father's wealth declined as steadily as his resentment of me grew." She wrapped arms around herself as though to shield her from the memory of her father's scorn. "Even then, he must have known of my intentions to run from him the moment I was able. He forced me to promise never to leave him without his consent."

And with the fae blood in her veins . . . "You are bound to honor your promises, like the fae?" Killian asked, shock in his voice.

But she was no pure-blooded fae.

"I'm not compelled to keep oaths, but breaking a promise could still result in chronic pain. A never-ending headache or a pervasive ache in the chest. Unless I wanted to spend the rest of my life in pain, I was forced to honor my promise. Await his permission to leave. But when I realized he intended to send me to the Keep . . . I knew I had to take matters into my own hands."

And here she was. Stranded on Prison Island. Leisa had been right to doubt her. Her sister knew Mailin threw caution to the wind when her mind was made.

Surprisingly, Killian didn't offer her words of sympathy. Instead, he reached out and drew her back against himself, holding her with a quiet understanding that soothed the ache in her chest far more than placating words.

After a few moments, he murmured, "You have never encountered your sisters since they were sold?"

Mailin shut her eyes and propped her cheek against his chest, listening to the soothing beat of his heart beneath her ears. "Only one. Leisa."

"Leisa?"

"She was bartered to a lord from the jade caste who fancied

young mistresses in exchange for land to expand the An Jin Estate."
Bitterness bled through her voice once more. "He was a mage of
old, close to three thousand summers. When he died, his wife sold
all his mistresses. Leisa ended up at Madam Sima's. I had hoped to
convince her to run away and follow me should I succeed in
securing Vale's proposal."

Killian's entire body stiffened. "Your *sister* . . . is a pleasure
worker at Madam Sima's?"

She nodded with a frown. He made an indeterminate grunt
in his throat, as though he were trying to form words he couldn't
seem to say.

Mailin narrowed her eyes. "What were *you* doing at Madam
Sima's that night?"

A foolish question. What other reasons did a man have for
visiting a brothel? Yet if he'd been Leisa's *client* . . .

Sickness greased her innards.

"Vale was there that night," he said haltingly, as though he
were afraid to speak. She didn't care a whit about where Vale was or
what he was doing that night.

"And you?" she prompted.

The guilt etched in his face nearly choked her until he told
her how he'd overdosed Vale with rexweed and spent the rest of the
night sleeping on the divan. Alone. Relief rushed through her so
acutely she released a near-hysterical laugh.

"You don't mind that he was . . . there?" He didn't need to
elaborate for her to guess whose patron Vale had been. She shook
her head with a sigh. "Leisa made her choice. Just as I made mine."

It rankled, but she had made her peace with Leisa's decision.
Perhaps one day, if she found the means to confidently offer her
sister a better life, she'd reach out to Leisa again. Until her own fate
was secured, she wouldn't look back. Now, her sight was fixed upon
the one man she knew she wanted in her future.

"So, you see, Killian Teranos," she murmured with a wry smile, "we aren't so different after all, you and I."

Two souls bearing scars of the past that had ultimately led them to each other.

FOURTEEN

KILLIAN

Killian roused when the sky was still black as pitch, but the telltale scent of dew saturating the air suggested dawn wasn't so far away. With his mind still ensnared in the fogginess of sleep, he burrowed his face into the nape of the warm woman nestled against his chest. She smelled like heaven and felt like sin.

He shifted slightly, hoping she wouldn't feel the part of him that seemed to have turned permanently to rock since she'd first touched him. Her eyes remained closed, her breathing slow and deep.

He looked down at her, trying to memorize the soft curve of her cheek, her petite nose, and the sensual bow shape of her lips.

For the first time, he saw beyond her class and title to the woman she was. A woman who knew blood, pain, and death, just as he did. She was right—they weren't so different after all. Where he bore scars on his skin, she bore them concealed beneath a lady's poise.

Yet she was also wrong.

A fundamental difference separated them. Where she'd done everything in her ability to free herself from her circumstances, Killian had done . . . nothing.

Unable to help himself, he ran a wayward finger down the bridge of her nose. Her lids fluttered and fanned open, and the corners of her lips lifted dreamily when her gaze found his. He smiled, as though he had every right to hold and touch her. He should let her go, but he didn't. Knave that he was, he only tightened his grip, allowing himself one more moment.

"Is it time to leave now?" she whispered, voice throaty.

He nodded as he brought the waterskin to her lips.

Never had he envied an inanimate object before, but now he wished he were the rim of the container. She handed it back to him, insisting he finish what was left. He shook his head. He would save it for her. The gods knew how long it would take for them to find the warden.

He drew her to her feet. As she fidgeted with her clothes, smoothing out her overlong shirt and adjusting the waistband of her stolen pants, Killian took the opportunity to stretch and think of his brother. Vale smoking too much rexweed, Vale intoxicated and taunting, Vale wielding a riding crop on both horses and women . . . The thoughts served to soften Killian's arousal so he could walk without chafing.

"I need to go." Her whispered words completely deflated his flesh. Did she mean to part ways with him? Here? Now?

She gave him a meaningful glance, pressing her legs together. When understanding dawned, Killian chuckled loud enough the sound bounced around them.

She glared at him, but followed readily as he led her from the tunnel.

Still shrouded in darkness, the woods were eerily quiet. No chirping insects. No whistling wind. The rustle of the undergrowth beneath their feet was the only sound competing with the sound of her own breathing. He found a spot suitably cloistered with tall-growing shrubs and nudged her toward it. "Here."

She wrinkled her little nose but nodded. "Can you . . . uh . . . go away?"

He acquiesced, stepping behind the bushes and turning his back for good measure. She didn't seem to appreciate his consideration.

"I can't do what I need to do with you standing right there!"

"I won't look," he promised.

"You'll . . . *hear.*" As though that were the worst possible thing that could befall her.

He grunted. "Just *go.*"

He heard her footsteps—funny how loudly such a small creature could stomp—then rustling bushes. Shuffling. More rustling. Then a loud, exasperated sigh. "I just can't."

If she thought he was going any further, she was sorely mistaken. His skin crawled just at not having her within his sights. "Would it help if I spoke? Then I won't be able to hear . . . uh . . . whatever you're doing."

"I don't need to be reminded you're standing less than five paces away." After another breath, she sighed. "I'll do the talking."

He grinned just as the first light of dawn rippled across the skies. "Whatever works, my lady." For the first time, he used her title as a tease.

With an audible huff, she began, but instead of speaking, she surprised him with a jocular tune.

"Twirl, twirl, little squirrel, swirl around like a dancing bear . . .
     Shy, shy little rabbit, skirting every clever snare . . ."

She started in a halting whisper, then her voice solidified, low enough it wouldn't carry too far, but loud enough to give her the false assurance he heard nothing but her singing.

"Jump, jump, little frog, leap over fences like a spotted cow . . .
Flutter, flutter, wing up north, don't flap about like a featherless owl . . .
Swim, swim, little fish, wiggle and waggle your fins for luck . . .
Giggle, giggle, little mouse, prance like a naughty pig in the muck . . .
Cry, cry, shed every sorrow, scaly snakes we do not fear . . .
Leap, leap, little goat, smile like a silly sheep is near . . .
Fall, fall, but don't stay down, pick yourself up like a little pink fawn . . .
Fly, fly, my scarlet swan, courage you will find at dawn . . ."

She repeated the song until she relaxed enough to do what she needed to do. Killian couldn't remember the last time he'd heard a lullaby. The cheerful tune was inane. Lighthearted. And oddly comforting. He found himself humming along under his breath even as he kept his senses alert for threats.

When she finally emerged, her cheeks sported charming pink flags to match the streaks of dawn coloring the skies.

He smirked, unable to resist. "Come along, scarlet swan. Time to fly."

Back at the polluted stream, Mailin trailed the embankment beside Killian, heading the direction the man claimed was northeast. How he could know which direction was which without a compass Mailin didn't know, but she posed no argument.

He could have led her to a slaughterhouse, and she would've followed him like a docile lamb.

She was far too tickled by the fact he was holding her firmly—almost possessively—by the hand with their fingers interlaced as he led her through twisting trees and craggy pathways.

"Are you sure we're not lost?" she quipped eventually, unable to help herself. Prolonged silence was not in her nature.

She received a noncommittal grunt. "That bald prisoner. Didn't the bastard mention newcomers cart ore through a valley to a tower where the warden lives?"

"Yes. But we don't know where the valley is, much less the direction of the tower."

He gave a contemplative nod of agreement. "We don't. But rivers usually run through valleys. If we follow this stream, we're likely to find the source of its pollution—the mines. Assuming the tower is what I think it is, it's probably built on higher terrain, likely to oversee the mines. With a little luck, we might just find the plateau where the tower is built. It shouldn't be hard to spot if we're in the valley."

Mailin blinked, impressed by his logic. "That . . . makes sense."

She replayed their conversation from the night before until the sun yawned to paint the skies in brilliant flashes of reds, pinks, and gold. She no longer desired to travel the realm, not when it meant leaving Killian behind. Yet she could never reside in Amereen, not if she were to be free. Would he truly help her escape his own brother? More, would he come *with* her?

A loud *crack* interrupted her thoughts.

Killian stiffened.

Two men charged through the underbrush. Killian shoved Mailin behind him so abruptly she staggered on her feet.

"Found them!" yelled one of the men.

"Yorn, they're over here!" hollered the other.

"Run!" Killian roared as he lunged forward, swinging a right hook that collapsed one man before he grappled with another. "Go, Mailin! I'll be right behind you!"

Confident Killian could handle two scrappy prisoners, she darted away. Getting herself caught would only hamper him. She followed the direction of the stream, her surroundings a smear of greens and browns. She slowed when she realized no one was coming after her.

No prisoners.

No Killian.

She whirled around, scanning the dense tree line, hoping to see a scarred bondsman emerge. Her heart ratcheted in her chest as time crawled by with no sign of the tall physique she desperately needed. *Follow the stream,* he had said. Follow the stream and it should lead them to the valley, and he believed the tower would be close by.

An agonized whimper escaped her throat. She didn't dare go back—what if she encountered more prisoners? Or worse, what if she found Killian . . . dead? Mailin pressed her fingers against her temples. He couldn't be. He'd slaughter the two before they could hurt him . . . but what if there had been more? What if—

Mailin started running.

She would find the warden—or die trying.

Railea must have heard her prayers, for soon the stream stretched into a river, and the ground grew steep. Finally, she understood why her bald attacker had referred to the valley as Dragon's Teeth. Flat slabs of rock jutted randomly from the escarpment, each one shaped distinctly like a jagged tooth. The scraggly rocks made the already steep incline even harder to climb.

She pushed forward, her heart a lump of dread in her chest and her legs trembling in trepidation. Time stretched to what seemed like hours, and adrenaline began to drain from her system, replaced by a bone-deep weariness.

Mailin leaned heavily against a boulder, scrubbing at her sweat-licked brow. A vicious pang of hunger struck in the form of nausea. She dry heaved, and her vision swam.

Goddess of mercy, she couldn't pass out now.

She blinked as a shadow marred the ground. Mailin glanced up. A sandstone monolith loomed over the canopy of trees, spearing the skies. She blinked.

The watchtower.

Hope exploded in her chest, displacing her lethargy.

She scrambled up the rocky incline to reach a plateau devoid of trees. Strange, glowing lines bisected the terrain. The Jirin Palace was similarly warded with a line of shimmering jade green etched in the ground. But these lines were gold. Amereen's color.

"Help," she cried, not daring to step over the golden boundary. "Help me, please!"

She could well be screaming into a void.

Mailin was a step away from the first line of shimmering gold when a man of considerable girth *materialized* from thin air right before her. She startled with a shriek and stumbled to the ground, jarring her tailbone. The man had warped. A teleporter.

"How dare you approach the watchtower?" The portly man snarled. He was garbed in a starched, white shirt of a noble official, the brass buttons straining to hold in his waistline. "I told you to leave the ore at the back end of the entrance and get—"

His forbidding frown turned to a gasp when he looked down at her. "A woman? Who are you?"

"I am no prisoner—" she managed before the air shimmered again.

A second man materialized into view. Even though she knew she was in the presence of yet another teleporter, Mailin couldn't help her gasp. She was not used to seeing men appear from thin air, and the effect put her in mind of fabled fae magic.

"What's the problem, Gideon?" This man was dressed far more formally than the first, in austere black from head to toe. The Amereenian gold buttons of his brocade shirtfront matched the epaulets fastened to his broad shoulders.

The stout official barely blinked at the second man's arrival. "Dar," he said, rubbing a fleshy hand at his eyes as though in disbelief. "Do my eyes deceive me, or does the lad look like a woman?"

"I *am* a woman!" Mailin shoved disheveled strands of hair from her face and pushed from the ground, jumping up to her full height. "Listen to me! I don't belong here!" Without prelude, she relayed the storm, her capsized dinghy, and waking up on the western shore of the island. She spoke so quickly she didn't know if her story was coherent, yet the men made no move to interrupt her. Gideon stared at her with his mouth partly agape while Dar's visage grew stern.

"You were in the company of the high mage Vale Teranos, you say?" Dar interjected.

Mailin nodded vigorously. "You must believe me," she pleaded. "You must help me. *Us*. Killian is still out there. I need to see the warden. I need—"

Gideon held out a placating hand and puffed out his chest. "There, there, little lady. I'll let you know that you are speaking to him. I *am* the warden. Gideon Mcfarlane, lord warden of the Isle of Groydon at your service." He nodded at the perpetually frowning Dar. "And this is Darragh, lord commander of Amereen's battlemages."

A whoosh of breath escaped Mailin's lips before she sank to her knees. "My lords, please. You must believe me."

When she glanced up, Gideon was scratching his hairless chin as he exchanged curious glances with the lord commander. A bout of silence stretched, and she knew they must be conversing telepathically. Silent speech was not unusual for mages powerful enough to teleport.

"We believe you, dear," the warden said. "No woman has been sentenced here for as long as I can remember."

"But Killian—" Mailin began, barely able to contain desperation in her voice.

Gideon held out another hand. "Fret not, my dear. We'll find this companion of yours—if he still lives."

S andwiched between Gideon and Darragh, Mailin was warped into what appeared to be the heart of the prisoners' camp. Her vision fractured and nausea rose up her throat. She staggered on her feet, but Gideon steadied her with a hand on her forearm.

Teleporting was a wholly unnerving experience, but the sound of boisterous men jeering quickly cleared her disconcertion. Prisoners crowded around a brawl.

"Clear it up, you hooligans," Gideon hollered, his voice booming over raucous shouts, clearing a path through the crowd.

A shout from a familiar, masculine voice caught her attention. Bolstered by the presence of the two lords who were clearly powerful enough to wander through an entire camp of bloodthirsty prisoners without a care, Mailin darted to the heart of the crowd just in time to see a man drive an uppercut into the scarred face that had become so dear to her.

She screamed and launched herself at Killian's attacker.

Hands grabbed at her.

Dimly, she heard Gideon growl, "Oh, for Railea's sake! Release the girl!"

When the prisoners did not comply, there was a loud crunch—the sound of snapping bones—and whoever had his hands on her staggered off. Gideon might appear homely and genial, but the warden was clearly lethal.

Painted in blood, sweat, and gore, Killian slammed a fist to his opponent's jaw as another prisoner tackled him from behind. They charged at him one or two at a time—as though in some sort of sick sport.

"Stop!" Mailin cried, but her screams faded in the rowdy crowd. One prisoner slammed into Killian from behind to strangle him with a chokehold as another delivered punches to his abdomen.

"In the name of Lord Archmage Thorne, you will cease this immediately!" Darragh boomed beside her, which seemed to startle every man in the vicinity to silence.

Everyone halted, except Killian, who took the opportunity to throw off his tackler and ram his knee into the man's throat.

"I said *stop*," Darragh yelled.

Killian paid him no heed. When his opponent went limp on the ground, he let out a guttural roar and punched him with enough force that an audible crack echoed.

"*Killian*," she shouted.

His fist stilled midair.

With a suppressed sob, Mailin pushed past gawking prisoners to throw her arms around his bloodied form. She ran her hands liberally over his face, his shoulders, and down his arms as she checked for wounds. He stared at her, his eyes wildly dilated.

"Mailin?" Then he grabbed her with such force she could hardly breathe.

"It's all right," she whispered, her healing energy pulsing between them. "I found him. I found the warden. We're safe now."

A shudder wracked his entire frame before he buried his face in the crook of her neck.

"You shouldn't be here." His breath whistled, his voice a broken rasp. "You should have stayed where it was safe."

She pressed her forehead against his bruised temple. "I am safest with you."

FIFTEEN

MAILIN

Mailin squeezed her eyes shut against the clamor and color of the capital to settle the queasiness in her gut. Being warped was disconcerting enough. Being warped twice in one day had her ready to heave.

"My lady?" At Killian's gentle murmur, Mailin freed herself from Darragh's grasp and tottered toward him. Killian lifted his arm as though to wrap it around her but promptly dropped it back to his side.

"Are you all right?"

Mailin nodded.

Gideon chuckled. "Warping is not for everybody. She'll feel better once the nausea passes." The lord warden shot Killian an appraising look. "You don't seem to suffer any ill effects, young man."

While the lord commander had ferried her, it was the lord warden who had teleported Killian. The four of them had materialized in the middle of a busy street where no one had batted an eyelash at their sudden appearance.

Clearly, the citizens of the Amereen capital were used to the coming and goings of the battlemages who served the court of Lord Archmage Thorne.

"I have a strong stomach," Killian mumbled, and the knob on his throat bobbed.

Mailin bit the insides of her cheek. Of course he felt no ill effects. If not for the metal collar suppressing his gifts, Killian would be a teleporter himself.

"My lady," said the lord commander. "I will take you directly to the Teranos Estate if you wish."

"No," Mailin blurted before she could think of a better retort.

At Darragh's frown, Mailin donned her most winsome smile. "Thank you for your kind offer, Lord Commander, but I will require some food and a change of clothes beforehand, you understand."

The furrow between Darragh's brows only deepened. "Your betrothed is a high mage of Amereen. Surely he is able to accommodate your every need."

"No, I couldn't possibly . . ." She gave a helpless shake of her head. "I couldn't possibly see him looking like this."

Killian stepped up to her side, his lips firm. "Lord Commander, I will make sure my lady returns to my lord's care safely—when she is ready."

The lord commander narrowed his eyes, his lips twisting into a sneer. "No one asked you for an opinion, bondsman."

Killian appeared unfazed by the commander's derogatory tone, but Mailin knew him well enough to see the affront leashed in his averted gaze.

Seeming satisfied with Killian's silence, Darragh turned back to Mailin. "My lady, I am certain that Lord Teranos is most certainly beside himself with worry."

Mailin bit down on her tongue before a scathing retort could leave her lips.

"Ah, Dar! This is why you remain an unmated man!" Gideon interjected with a knowing smile. "Can't you see what's happening here?"

Beside her, Killian stiffened. Mailin swallowed the lump in her throat. Bleeding skies, she'd all but thrown herself into Killian's arms before.

The warden gave a dismissive wave. "No woman wants to appear before her betrothed looking like she's been dragged through the mud. On Prison Island, no less!" Gideon gave a hearty chuckle. "Everyone knows of Lord Teranos's reputation. Imagine asking her to make her first appearance before his servants, looking like . . . this."

Mailin nodded fervently. "Oh, Lord Warden, you're absolutely right." She gestured at her clothes and donned her haughtiest expression. "I fear if Lord Teranos sees me in this manner, he may even be tempted to annul our betrothal. I'll need a bath, fresh clothes, a lady to tend to my hair . . ."

The lord commander's eyes began to glaze as she nattered on about undergarments and her other womanly needs before interjecting, "Very well. If you feel so strongly, my lady, I shall direct you to a local bathing parlor where you can make yourself presentable. Meanwhile, the bondsman and I shall make our way to Lord Teranos's estate to deliver the news of your safety."

"No!" The very thought of being separated from Killian wrought something close to panic in her chest.

The lord commander blinked. "I can't possibly leave you wandering in the capital under the care of a bondsman, my lady."

Mailin folded her arms. "This bondsman kept me alive the last two days, Lord Commander. I would have suffered a fate far worse had it not been for him." She pursed her lips for added effect.

"Besides, a few hours in a bathing parlor will hardly suffice. Have you seen the condition of my nails, my lord?" She held her fingers up to his face. "Do you know how long I'll need to soak myself before I can purge the dirt from my pores?"

Gideon cleared his throat, a smirk twitching his lips. "There now. Fret not, my lady. How about this? We will find you a suitable inn where you'll get all your feminine needs tended to."

"And I will send word to my lord first thing in the morning," Killian added.

Gideon beamed. "Yes. Yes, a fine plan." He rifled in his pockets and produced several coins—gold pieces, not copper jaroobis—and pressed them into Mailin's hands. "These should be enough to buy you what you need, my dear."

Mailin blinked. There was enough coin to purchase an entire trousseau. "I can't possibly—"

Gideon gave a cavalier shrug. "I won't hear it, my dear. You've given me quite enough amusement for years to come." He gave her forearm a fatherly pat before he turned to regard Killian. "I trust she is in good hands, lad?"

Killian nodded. "I will guard her with my life, my lord."

Mailin stared at the coins in her hands. She closed her fingers over them and clutched them close to her chest. "Lord Warden, I don't know how I'll ever repay you."

Gideon smiled. "Might I suggest taking a long soak and a good night's sleep?" He surprised her by leaning closer to her ear as he lowered his voice. "The hardest decisions are best made with a clear head."

He drew the baffled looking Darragh away by the forearm. "Come along Dar. I'm sure the poor lady is eager for some rest. Now, on this rare occasion I'm here . . . why don't you show me your favorite place for a pint?"

The lord commander turned to pin Killian with a glare. "You

will call for Lord Teranos at *first* light."

While Killian nodded at the commander, Gideon gave Mailin a parting wave and shot her a sly wink. "Good luck, my dear."

Unease lined Mailin's gut when Killian fell into silence as soon as they parted ways with the lord warden and the lord commander. Not only did he maintain a distance between them, but he also steered her straight to a modest-looking tavern, further crushing her spirits.

Some small part of her had hoped he would take her to the Traveling Wagons, where he would declare his intentions to elope.

Instead, he commandeered Gideon's coins as he ordered two separate rooms and a hot meal for them both. He even gave the taverner's wife—Saoire, a rosy-cheeked woman with a charming gap-toothed smile—specific orders to procure Mailin a dress and any other items she might need to make her "presentable."

Mailin climbed woodenly up the creaky stairwell as the matron led them to their rooms. Hers was surprisingly spacious and sparse, dominated by a four-poster bed with clean sheets smelling of fresh verbena. A fire crackled merrily at a small hearth.

Killian hovered by the doorway, still wearing an indecipherable expression. On her way out the door, Saoire passed Killian the key to his own room. At the matron's departing footsteps, a near feverish intensity bled into his eyes.

"Mailin."

She darted forward wordlessly, and he met her in the middle of the room to swoop her into his arms. A shudder of relief wracked her frame.

His mouth traversed her cheek, leaving a trail of clandestine kisses in its wake. When his lips found hers, Mailin melted against the heat of his mouth with a moan.

Killian's kisses had been sweet and soft. Gentle, with a hint of reverence. This time, however, it was ravenous and rough, filled with tongue and teeth . . . Almost punishing. They were both panting when he pulled away.

He dipped his head and brought their foreheads together, staring as though he were trying to memorize every detail of her face. He grazed her cheek with a hand, tender and trembling.

Mailin frowned. "What's wrong?"

Yearning and desire were etched into every line of his face, yet his gaze . . . Dread spiderwebbed in her chest.

His eyes were filled with regret.

He took a step back. The small distance between was as punishing as the wards encircling Prison Island. He shuffled over to the tiny bedside table, rummaging through his pockets to produce what was left of Gideon's coins and set them on top.

He retreated to the door, stubbornly avoiding her gaze.

"Killian?" she whispered, her voice brittle.

Slowly, he lifted his eyes to meet hers, his eyes brimming with anguish and an unspoken apology. "I will leave for the Teranos Estate at dawn. That will give you plenty of time to get to the Traveling Wagons at the end of this street."

Her lips parted; her jaw slackened.

"Be happy, Mailin."

Then he was gone, leaving her standing in the middle of the room, bewildered and bereft. Mailin sucked in a breath. The air sliced into her lungs like a sharpened blade, tearing and twisting in her chest.

He couldn't possibly mean to leave her. Not after all they'd been through.

She stalked to the door just as a rap sounded.

Her heart soared.

She threw open the door, expecting a scarred man with a change of heart. Instead, Saoire wheeled in a large, wooden tub, followed by two young men carting buckets of steaming water. A maid came in last, holding a timber tray laden with fresh bread, roasted meats, and a generous serving of gravy.

Saoire handed her a white bathrobe that had been tucked under her arm. "It'll be a little while before my girl returns from the dressmaker with fresh clothes for you. Meanwhile, I thought you might find this more comfortable after your bath."

Mailin accepted the soft robe with a strained smile. "Thank you, Saoire."

And she was once again left to her lonesome. A hearty dinner and a hot bath. She should be thrilled. Freedom was now well within her reach, yet she felt numb. Hollow.

She latched the door and turned to the food platter. She stuffed an entire slice of roast beef in her mouth and chewed ferociously. Why should she chase after him like an abandoned pup? His decision was clear—he didn't want her. She bit off a large chunk of bread, and her stomach threatened to rebel.

Funny how food tasted so bland even though she'd starved for two long days.

Ironic how she'd formed such an attachment to a man in two short days.

Her gaze went to the gold coins on the table.

Be happy, Mailin, he had said. A pang struck her heart. Killian had given her time to eat, an opportunity to bathe, a warm bed to sleep in, and time to escape. But he'd never intended to elope with her.

She sipped more of the sweet mead, but only tasted the salt of her own tears.

He was not a true bondsman. He wore the collar by choice,

paying a penance he did not owe. Who was she to convince him otherwise? Had she truly thought he would give up his life, his brother, for her?

He was right. She should forget him. She would go to the wagons at first light. A bitter sound escaped her throat, a cross between a hysterical laugh and a sob. She was finally free, yet her heart was no longer her own.

She stripped off her filthy clothes. The memory of Killian stripping on the beach and offering her the shirt off his back haunted her mind, further twisting her heart. She clutched the rough fabric, hands fisting.

She tossed the shirt into the fire and stared with impassioned eyes as the flames devoured her offering.

She climbed into the tub with the finesse of a stomping child, sloshing water onto the ground. She grabbed the bar of precious soap and lathered her hair, then scrubbed angrily at every inch of her skin. As the water cooled, her anger heated to a boil.

Who in the five hells did he think he was, holding and kissing her in that manner and then telling her to *"be happy"*? She had tasted his desire, sensed his yearning.

Blast the man. The bastard wanted her as much as she did him.

With a huff, she pushed from the tub and wiped herself dry. Her stolen prison garb was now cinders in the flames, so she yanked on the bathrobe and stormed out her door, nearly flattening Saoire in her haste.

"My lady." The matron held up a brown package. "Fresh clothes that should fit you."

Mailin accepted it gratefully and turned to toss the package into her room. Before the taverner's wife could retreat, Mailin quickly blurted, "Saoire, but can you, um, tell me which room Killian is in?"

The matron's brows winged up as she stared pointedly at Mailin's bathrobe, then at her flaming cheeks. Then again, what did her reputation matter? She would be gone at dawn.

Saoire directed her to the door marked *seven*, and Mailin thanked her with as much dignity as she could muster. She pounded a furious fist at Killian's door.

The door opened a fraction to show the scarred portion of his face. How fitting—the side of him he wore as shame and used as a shield.

His lips parted at the sight of her, but Mailin didn't give him a chance to speak. She shoved the door wide open and marched brazenly into his room. It was significantly smaller than hers, with a single cot pressed against the wall.

Killian eyed her warily, running a hand through soaked hair. A large bucket sat by the hearth, and several soiled washcloths were strewn on the ground. A pang struck her chest. He hadn't even ordered himself a proper bath.

"You shouldn't be in here, my lady."

She shot him a sour glance. "So now I'm once again your lady?"

Mailin crossed her arms. He didn't meet her gaze, keeping his sights on the ground as though the wooden slats were more interesting than she.

Perhaps sheer anger emboldened her, or perhaps it was surviving a storm, or escaping Prison Island. Perhaps she was simply tired of Killian's self-deprecating attitude. Tired of his refusal to take what they *both* wanted. Mailin undid the sash around her waist and let her robe fall to the floor.

His head snapped up, his eyes bulging. He slapped both hands over his face to cover his eyes like a horrified child.

"Railea's blood! What are you doing?"

If she couldn't have forever with him, she would settle for

one night. One night before they parted ways at dawn. One night to remember a man who would forever have first claim to her heart. He might as well have first claim to her body.

She moved to stand before him and placed a palm on his broad chest. He shivered, and she smirked. She tugged his hands away from his face, but his eyes remained stubbornly shut.

"Put it back on," he commanded, but his tone lacked authority. "Mailin, do you hear me? I said—"

She rolled her eyes and pressed herself close, wrapping her arms around his waist.

His eyes sprang open at her contact, then he stumbled back like a newborn fawn, nearly toppling the jug of water on the dresser. His gaze landed upon her, latched onto her breasts, and suddenly he couldn't stop staring.

"Gods, Mailin." His voice was a husky whisper, her name uttered like a plea.

"I want you, Killian," she murmured. "I know you want me, too."

"Why?" he asked, his eyes darting from her face to her breasts and back again. With what appeared to be valiant effort, he plastered his sight to the ceiling. "If you want to thank me for the last two days, I—"

She rose to the tip of her toes, her breasts brushing against the soft cotton of his shirt, to press her lips against his bearded jaw.

"This isn't about gratitude," she said. "This is about how I've felt from the very first moment I saw you." An attraction that had solidified into something that scared even her, but Mailin had always been one to wear her heart on her sleeve. "This is about what I feel for *you*."

His body was strung taut like a sail at full mast, tension thrumming off every inch of his powerful frame. She grinned at the rapid rise of his chest and the firm clench of his jaw. What would it take for his restraint to snap?

"One night. That's all I'm asking for." Mamma had wasted her life on a heartless man. Mailin wouldn't waste hers wondering what it would be like to be with the man who held her heart.

He squeezed his eyes shut again, as though it pained him to look at her. "You deserve more than this." He ground the words between his teeth. The veins on the side of his neck stark against his skin, like the scar on his face. "You deserve a man who can give you everything you've ever dreamed of. I am not that man. I have nothing to give."

"Liar," she whispered.

He didn't budge. He didn't open his eyes.

"Look at me," she commanded, "and tell me you don't want me."

He obeyed, and she found herself lost in a pair of rich brown eyes flecked with the hue of golden barley, filled with suppressed desire and unspoken wants.

"It does not matter what I want. The only thing that matters is what you deserve. And you deserve more than a tryst with a man who has nothing to offer."

"Then don't make it a tryst." She laid a hand on his chest, willing him to look at her. Willing him to *choose* her, as she'd chosen him. She risked the final remnants of her dignity and added, "You are everything I want."

He finally met her gaze, his eyes wide with disbelief. "A powerless bondsman is everything you want? A man who does nothing but his brother's bidding?" He curled his lips. "Go back to your room, Mailin."

Mailin released a mirthless laugh and let her hand fall from his chest, her cheeks flaming as though she'd been rouged with hot coals. Humiliation welled to suffuse the cracks of her wounded pride, but it was disappointment that caused her voice to waver.

"You're not powerless." She stepped back from him, her poise jerky as she donned her discarded robe. "But you're a coward. The only thing holding yourself back is you."

He flinched as though she'd slapped him, yet his eyes remained downcast. "I'm sorry."

She held her chin high. "So am I. Goodbye, Killian Teranos."

SIXTEEN

KILLIAN

As Mailin disappeared through the door, Killian fisted his hands to stop himself from punching a hole in the wall. Startling heat prickled at the back of his eyes. He blinked rapidly, drawing in deep breaths. He felt as though he'd just ripped out a part of his heart.

It was for the best. She deserved better; she deserved more.

Mailin was smart and resourceful. She could take care of herself. She could earn a decent living for herself, scrap-healing as she traveled from town to town, province to province. He didn't doubt she could disappear in the way of nomads and live her dreams.

All she needed was a chance to escape, and freedom was the *one* thing he could give her.

And he damn well would.

Gods, he wanted nothing more than to flee with her, but that was a fool's dream. Now the lord commander was privy to their whereabouts, Vale would eventually learn the truth of their survival, and his brother would not let them go without retribution. No. Killian knew his brother far too well. Vale would scour the realm until he found them, no matter the years it took.

Eloping with Mailin would not only commit her to a lackluster existence, but it would also condemn her to a lifetime of running.

But if Killian remained, he could—and he *would*—sabotage Vale's every move to find her, and safeguard her freedom. With a little time and ingenuity, he'd find a way to feed Vale a well-fabricated lie of her unfortunate demise.

Mailin would then be free to live her life. To live her dreams.

Eventually, she'd find a decent place to settle and forget all about him. An ache formed in his chest like a festering rot. She'd find another man more worthy of her affections, some lucky bastard who would have the right to touch and claim her for his own. All while Killian continued with his wretched existence, where he would agonize every minute of every day for the rest of his life over her safety. Her wellbeing. Her happiness.

Insidious thoughts formed in his mind, taunting his decisions. What if Mailin was mistreated? What if she got involved with a man who abused her the way Vale did his whores when he smoked too much rexweed? What if she came upon backwater settlements filled with seedy merchants and cutthroat mercenaries . . . or worse, the fae slave operators rumored to abduct women?

Sickness coagulated in his gut, and strain pulsed between his temples. Could he trust any other man to cherish her the way he did, protect her the way he would? Could any other man love her the way he did?

He swallowed. *Love.* Did he truly?

More, did he dare?

You're everything I want. Her words returned to haunt him, and he knew they would for the rest of his life.

Commotion sounded outside the hallway, interrupting his jumbled thoughts. A muted quarrel between a drunk-sounding man and a woman.

Mailin.

Killian sprang to his feet and charged through the door and into the hallway just in time to see Mailin deliver a sound slap to a leering lout.

"Piss off," she shouted.

The man glowered. "Railea's teeth, woman! Then why run around dressed like that?"

Killian prowled up to them without suppressing the growl in his throat.

The man took one look at him and scurried off, rubbing a hand against his reddened cheek. Mailin caught sight of Killian and veered for her door.

In that moment, everything became startlingly *clear*. The miasma of his thoughts—his fears, his reservations, his yearnings, his desire—it all unraveled as though he'd been treading through fog the whole time and the sun had finally risen.

Killian caught her by the wrist and shoved her back against the wall. He caged her between his arms in a position not so different from their first encounter in the back alley of Madam Sima's.

She batted at his chest. "What are you doing? You've made yourself clear. I understand."

"No," he growled. "No, you don't."

When he didn't budge, she glared at him in a way that made him wary. It wouldn't be the first time the little firebrand attempted to knee him in the balls. "You're right. I am a coward."

A good start, for it wiped the glower from her face.

"I *want* you, Mailin." He lowered his head so she could see directly into his eyes. He no longer wanted to hide. "I want you. I want you with every fiber of my being, with every waking thought of my mind. I want you so completely, so desperately I would happily bleed myself dry if I could even be a fraction of the man you deserve."

She blinked rapidly, her lips parting and closing. "Wha . . . what changed your m-mind?"

Killian smiled at her uncharacteristic stutter. "A wise woman once told me never to wait for someone else to do something I can do for myself." He drew in a deep, shuddering breath, gathering his courage. "I may be a coward, but I am no fool. I won't stand by and wait for another man to do what I so desperately want to. Not when I know without a doubt no other man in all the five realms could yearn for you, want you, worship you the way *I* do." He swallowed. "I may never give you everything you deserve, Mailin, but I swear to the gods right here, right now, that I will strive to give you everything you need, everything you want."

She stared at him, strangely silent.

The moment was shattered as one of the tavern boys scurried past them with a tray of empty dishes in his hand and curiosity on his face. Mailin ducked her head. A pretty flush colored her cheeks before she murmured, "All right."

Her response was too obscure for his liking.

Killian tipped her chin up so he could scour her gaze for answers he so desperately needed. "Do you still want me, Mailin?"

She offered him a shy smile, the curve on her lips almost tipsy, as though she'd imbibed far too much spirits. "Yes, Killian. *Yes.*"

Killian increased the pressure of his grip and gave her a tiny shake to emphasize the gravity of his query. "I'm not asking if you'll have me for this one night. I'm asking if you'll have *me.*"

He would not tumble her on the sheets for a night of

forbidden passion. He meant every word he'd said. She deserved more. She deserved a life as bright, brilliant, and beautiful as her spirit . . . as well as a man who would cater to her every whim and want.

He was not that man.

He had no longer access to his wealth nor noble title, but everything else he had, everything else he was, he would lay at her feet—his devotion, his desire, his heart. Along with a promise to spend the rest of his life striving to be the man she deserved.

Her eyes glimmered.

Killian's heart thudded hard against his ribcage. "Mailin . . . ?"

She bowed her head—this woman of indomitable spirit and a steel spine—and burrowed into his chest, claiming a space that could never be filled by another.

"Make love to me, Killian," she whispered, lighting a fire in his soul with her words. "Make me yours."

Mailin's pulse heightened as Killian's eyes darkened in response to her bold words. She swallowed. *Make me yours,* she'd said. His. All her life Mailin had yearned to escape possession—from societal expectations of her halfbreed abilities, from her father's oppression, from a possible life at the Keep. Now she wanted nothing more than to belong to this one man.

"Mine," he murmured. The following rumble from his throat caused her legs to tremble and heat to simmer at her core. Mailin wanted him to peel back her robe, to run his callused hands all over her skin. Impatience had her rising to the tip of her toes the same time he dipped his head.

Their foreheads collided.

"Ow!" Laughing, Mailin tilted her head to give him better access, but eagerness gave him bad timing. His nose smacked into her temple.

With a disgruntled huff, Killian captured her cheeks between his hands. His grip was unyielding, and his thumb rubbed at the spot he'd bumped, his gaze infinitely tender. Mailin was still giggling when his mouth descended over hers, but she quickly sobered when his tongue delved deep.

She sighed into his mouth and wrapped her hands around his shoulders to pull him closer. He surprised her by lifting her off her feet as though she weighed no more than a child. Instinctively, Mailin parted her legs to secure them around his hips. There was no escaping the bulge in his pants, which pressed insistently against her, rousing equal measures of excitement and apprehension. She had healed plenty of men and seen unclothed male anatomy too often to be a shy innocent, but it appeared her chosen lover was rather well-endowed.

She'd spent enough time at Madam Sima's to know that large meant more pain, especially for the first time. But this was Killian. She would take anything he was willing to give.

With their lips still fused and their tongues still tangled, they ignored a gasp from a passing patron. Mailin was barely aware of him walking them both into her room. She was so intoxicated by his taste that she barely registered the *snap* of the door latch before Killian pinned her to the wall, as though the four paces to the bed were too far for him.

One large hand supported her weight while the other snaked beneath her robe to mold her breast, the roughness of his skin a thrilling contrast to the gentleness of his touch. He toyed with her nipple, teasing the hardened nub between his thumb and forefinger with his gaze rapt on her face, drinking in her every expression. He paused at every hitch of her breath only to repeat the motion, as though he were trying to memorize each move.

"Killian," she pleaded, though she wasn't exactly sure what she wanted. The man already had her back plastered to the wall, his body pinning hers, his hands fondling, and his lips grazing her skin. But she simply wanted *more*.

More kisses. More caresses. Just more Killian.

He responded by settling her back on her legs.

"No . . ." She wanted to be closer, not set down. He promptly silenced her when he bent to part her robe with his *face* and replaced the fingers caressing her nipple with his tongue. He resumed his exploration with the deliberation of an artist, using his tongue like a brush, painting her breast with fervent kisses and lusty bites. A moan rose from her throat while the dampness between her legs intensified . . . but he was barely finished with one breast. With the same maddening deliberation, he worked his way to the soft underside, seemingly intent on titillating her to insanity.

"*Killian*," she gasped.

He chuckled against her skin, and the vibrating sound wrung more slickness between her legs. Finally he lifted his head to meet her eyes, the intensity in his gaze feverish as he slid one hand southward to stroke her slick core.

Her thighs quivered as his large hand explored the part of her that had never been touched. If he hadn't had her pinned to the wall, she would have toppled over from the rioting sensations.

"You like this," he murmured, wonderment in his eyes as though he could hardly believe he was giving her such pleasure. She could hardly believe it herself. She was panting, a near mindless creature with the wanton urge to grind herself against the apex of his palm. When he brushed long fingers against her slick and needy flesh, Mailin barely recognized the sound that came from her throat, a sort of gasping mewl she'd never thought she could make.

His wonderment morphed into a grin as he hastened his

motions, trying to wring more sounds of pleasure from her throat.

Mailin reached for the fasteners at his waistband. "I want to see you." She wanted to—needed to—give him the same pleasure. To touch him the way he touched her.

The ardent haze in his eyes ebbed to uncertainty. "I . . . my body isn't a beautiful sight, Mailin."

She flattened her lips, a surge of hate rising for the guardians who had marred such a magnificent man. No matter. She would remedy his misconceptions. She tugged at his shirt, eager and insistent. She had the rest of their lives to show him exactly how beautiful he was.

Slowly, almost reluctantly, he complied and pulled off his shirt. He visibly held his breath as her scrutiny wandered over the ropy lines crisscrossing his bare chest.

"There is nothing beautiful about the savagery that's been done to you." Mailin leaned forward and gently pressed her lips just below his collarbone, where a white furrow lacerated his skin. His breath grew short, and his pectoral muscle twitched beneath her fingers.

Her voice broke. "I *hate* the pain you endured when these were carved into your skin." She proceeded to trace every scar she could find with her fingertips, ravenous in her quest to learn every spectacular part of him. "But you are a beautiful man, Killian Teranos, and believe me: these scars only make you . . . more.

"More beautiful," she purred, rubbing herself against him. "More intriguing." She continued downward, tracing the scar with her lips until she was almost on her knees, kissing the jagged lines on his abdomen, drawing a hissed breath from his throat. "Perfect."

E lation buoyed up in his chest until it burst, and euphoria bubbled through his blood. Her words slayed something in him. They destroyed the bitter self-condemnation that had held him captive, freeing him from a prison that he'd believed had no key. All thoughts of his scars, his collar, and his indenture faded from his mind. He would deal with it all in the morning. Right this moment, he would deny her—and himself—no longer.

No longer apprehensive, no longer hesitant, he pulled her up from her knees and lifted her off her feet once more.

She emitted a sound of protest. "I'm not done kissing you."

A shudder wracked him. Gods, if she kissed him *there* he would probably combust and embarrass them both. "Soon," he promised. His voice had grown so husky it sounded guttural to his own ears.

Cradling his precious cargo, he took care to lay her on the bed. She was a prize he'd done nothing to win but would spend the rest of his life cherishing.

She allowed him to undo the rest of her bathrobe, her eyes warm, her body pliant as he exposed every inch of her to his eager gaze.

She was perfection manifested in the form of a woman, from the crown of her head down to her dainty toes. Like a man in a trance, he planted one knee on the edge of the bed as he lowered himself to better ogle the mouthwatering curve of her quivering breasts, the dip of her narrow waist, and the soft flare of her hips.

He skimmed a knuckle over her cheek to her collarbone, then teased over the rise of her chest to trace the peak. He frowned. He'd already left little bruises on the one breast he'd feasted upon. He would have to be gentler.

She didn't seem to agree.

She tugged at his shoulders, urging him down with her soft whimpers and kneading hands so that Killian could no longer think.

He could only feel. And he felt feverish, as though his pants had been set afire. With an eagerness he'd only ever felt as a child on the morning of Harvest Day, he shucked his pants with a swiftness which rounded both her eyes and lips.

"*Oh*," she whispered, and the awe in her eyes caused more than just his confidence to swell. Grinning like a fool, he clambered over her.

The mattress protested their collective weight with a low *creak*. The crude sound caused him to pause.

Though she looked up at him with open desire, her skin was flushed with shyness and her fingers twisted knots in the sheets. He felt like a clumsy beast about to crush a blushing rose.

"I've never been with a woman before," he blurted, and instantly wanted to kick himself for the awkward admission.

The only women he'd attempted had been Vale's whores, and even then, their thinly veiled disgust at the scars on his body had doused his desires. Nothing dampened ardor like knowing the women were only willing for the sake of coin.

"Well, you're my first, too, so I don't know what to expect." Soft, solemn words but mischief lit her eyes as her sight traveled down to his hardened length resting heavily against her belly. "I reckon you're setting quite a high bar."

Though her words stroked his ego the same way her fingers stroked his biceps, he scowled. "You'll never test the bar with another."

He'd kill any man who tried.

Her answering giggle relieved the tension in his muscles. "My first and only."

Pacified, he resumed his cautious exploration, caressing and fondling until her legs fell apart, and he settled instinctively between her thighs. The basest part of him had hardened to the point of pain, pulsing with the need to plunder.

In the past, he'd taught himself to release quickly. A few rapid pumps of his hand and he was done with his basic urges. Now he wanted so desperately to go slow, to sip every kiss and savor every touch. Yet, she seemed determined to test his resolve as she writhed beneath him, wondrously wanton, and he prayed he wouldn't disappoint her.

He licked and laved, kissed and nibbled, feasting his fill, pausing whenever her sighs turned to strangled moans just so he could repeat the motions, eager to learn all her erogenous secrets. When he finally nudged against her slick opening, she filled the room with an erotic litany of incoherent moans, her nails scraping down his back, her hips rolling to take him in.

He covered her lips with his, drinking in her impassioned cries as he slid into her inch by slow inch, until he was the one groaning with irrepressible pleasure.

"*Mailin.*" He groaned, unable to stop himself from chanting her name when he was fully sheathed within her tight channel. Through sheer will he didn't know he possessed, he refused himself immediate release, relishing the symphony of their bodies conjoined until he found the spot that made her clench and convulse. He lost all semblance of control. He pounded ceaselessly between her thighs, needing to give her more. To give her everything. His name was a fervent cry on her lips when he gave one final thrust and followed her over the edge.

K illian turned his back to the sunlight streaming through the windows and buried his face in the crook of Mailin's neck, his body steeped in leisure and lassitude.

Drawing in a deep breath of the fragrance of her skin, he

sighed with a smile. Never in his wildest dreams had he imagined sharing his body with a woman who wasn't repulsed by his scars but aroused by them.

And not just any woman, but *Mailin*. A woman who had lavished every scar on his body with such meticulous attention and fervent adoration that she vanquished all notion of his inadequacies. He tightened his arms around her slender frame and ran his fingers through the choppy strands of her midnight tresses.

Her hair lay in silken ribbons around her head, competing with her lashes to feather over the curve of her cheek. She was partially turned on her side, and the shell of one dainty ear—ever so slightly pointed at the tip to whisper of her fae heritage—peeked from her hair.

A halfbreed in his bed.

A heady compulsion rose in his chest. Not the urge to rut, though that was growing into a pervasive ache in his loins. It was the urge to *mate*. To intertwine their psyches and bind his life to hers.

The yearning was so strong it frightened him.

He had never thought he'd have the desire to take an elorin de ana, but now he yearned to be the man she called elorin de han. He traced the curve of her breast down to the soft dip of her abdomen, cataloguing the small, reddened patches he'd left across her skin. His passion had run astray last night, but she hadn't complained. More, she'd urged him on.

He proceeded to kiss every mark he could find, and his flesh hardened in anticipation. After their first time, he'd managed to coax entry into her twice more before she fell into a deep sleep. Would she allow him in again so soon?

With her eyes still closed, she released a drowsy "Mmm."

The fatigue in her tone gave him pause.

"How are you feeling?" Killian rolled her to her back so he could better study her expression, but she didn't open her eyes. Had he overtired her? Or worse. "Have I hurt you?"

Her eyelids lifted along with the corners of her lips to soothe the anxiety rising in his chest. "Silly man. I feel absolutely wonderful." Her hands stroked him from cheek to chest. "What about you?" Her hands dipped lower, her smile taking a seductive slant. "How do *you* feel?"

Killian grinned wide and proceeded to show her exactly how he felt.

He was ready to drive himself home when a rude, insistent rap at the door interrupted him. Killian groaned. He'd ordered breakfast the previous night. Mailin giggled at his obvious disappointment as she shimmied and snuck beneath the counterpane. With a sigh, Killian yanked on his pants—no easy feat—and shirt before he opened the door.

The taverner's wife waited patiently with a tray of thinly sliced, smoked meats and crusty bread. Then he noticed the large bucket at her feet. His brows furrowed. He hadn't ordered or paid for a second wash bucket.

Saoire, clearly reading his frown, leaned closer and slapped fresh washcloths into his hand. "On the house, lad. The lady will be wanting a wash."

Killian accepted her offering with a grin, too delirious to feel embarrassed. After latching the door shut, he left the breakfast tray on the bedside table and Saoire's offering on the ground. No sense cleaning up when he fully intended to smirch *the lady* once more.

The water and food were both cold by the time he allowed Mailin out of the bed, but she raised no complaints. When they were both satisfactorily clean, Killian heartily devoured his breakfast, but Mailin fidgeted with her food.

"Killian," she began, the uncertainty in her tone causing him to frown. "Last night . . ." She picked at the bread's crust, as though choosing her words carefully. "I know I pushed you to a decision, but I want you to know I won't hold you to it." Her voice wavered, unusually meek. "If you change your mind . . ."

"Are you asking me if I still want you to leave?" he asked, annoyed she was doubting his intent. Hadn't he made himself clear last night? He leaned over to grip her chin so she met his gaze. "Make no mistake, Mailin, I have no intention of ever letting you go. You're mine now."

The relief on her face only heightened his annoyance.

"I don't want you to feel like you need to stay with me out of obligation . . . or responsibility."

He stared at her in disbelief. Did she think he would bed her then send her packing the next morning like some common whore?

"You're not an obligation. You're the very thing I've always wanted but never thought I could ever have. Mailin, you're my dream come true."

His response seemed to satisfy her for a dreamy smile returned to her lips, and she curled up beside him, her head fitting perfectly into the crook of his neck. "Am I?"

"You are." He pulled her in for a kiss so she would never mistake herself for anything less.

When he released her lips, her smile was so vibrant it was almost incandescent. "Well then, where shall we go? Not too far north since you dislike the cold," she paused, her brows puckering in consideration. "Batuhan might be nice. We'll find a small, obscure village. Preferably one populated by humans. They know to mind their own business, so they won't question your collar." She shot him a cheery glance. "I'll scrap-heal, while you find some local work." She clasped her hands together with glee. "One day, we'll save enough to buy our own land, grow our own crops. Doesn't that sound nice?"

If his heart hadn't already melted the night before, it would have puddled at her feet at that moment. He caught her face between his hands and stole another kiss. She had remembered their conversation and painted their future with *his* dreams. He would be happy living in an obscure village, plowing the fields by day, and even happier plowing between her legs at night. But what of her dreams?

He wanted so much more for her. He wanted to give her a life filled with color and purpose to suit her vivacious spirit. He wanted to show her the glaciers of Flen, the sand dunes of Teti Unas, and the ranges of Batuhan. He didn't want her to live a mundane life as a farmer's wife. He told her as much.

She shook her head. "I don't need any of those things, Killian. As long as we're together, I'll be the happiest woman in the realm."

His heart threatened to burst from his chest. The things this woman made him *feel* . . . He would do right by her. He would not have her settle for anything less than the best he could offer, and he could offer a lot more if he were unhindered by his collar.

"Vale needs to be persuaded to remove my bond." A bonded collar could only be unlocked with blood. As it was Vale's blood that had sealed the bond, it could only be Vale that set him free.

Mailin crawled onto his lap, her lips pursed in a wry curve. "I have not known your brother long, but I do not think he will agree to set you free quite so easily."

Killian gave a sad nod. "Not without some coercion; he wouldn't."

"But why?"

"Vale went considerable lengths to ensure I'd never reclaim my inheritance. He dismissed and replaced staff and even threatened to exile the Teramaine farmers should they acknowledge me. He worked hard to erase my identity from memory." Killian sagged his shoulders, suddenly overcome with shame.

Killian made Vale sound like a villain, but was he not

equally culpable? He had *allowed* his brother to do those things. He had put up with Vale's mistreatment and even cast a blind eye to his brother's transgressions because, in a perverse way, Killian had equated it all to penance. The worse Vale treated him, the more he felt he'd atoned. He'd hidden behind the mask of Scar for far too long, and it took a free-spirited woman who saw past his insecurities to help him see how blind he'd been. It was time Scar came to an end so Killian Teranos could live.

"But we are a long-lived people," Killian murmured. "The staff of the Teranos household might have been replaced, but the vicegerents of the small towns in Teramaine all know who the true Teranos heir is, as do most of those who've lived in the town."

The rich lands of Teramaine had been passed down from one Teranos heir to the next for generations. It was the reason Vale sent Killian for most of his dealings with the small-town officials. The people might know him as Vale's appointed bondsman, yet they hadn't forgotten he was the firstborn.

Mailin pushed from his chest with her mouth agape. "You plan to rally support from the masses and challenge Vale for your inheritance?"

Killian frowned. "I plan to rally support, yes, but not to reclaim my inheritance. I only wish to push Vale to see reason and free me from this collar." He had never dreamed of regaining control of the Teramaine lands. Vale might be petty and perverse. Cruel, even, when it came to Killian, but the high mage had never been remiss in the management of their lands. Teramaine thrived under Vale's hand, which had, in a way, fed Killian's complacency. He didn't care who manned the helm, so long Teramaine flourished.

"Do you . . . wish to be Lady Teranos?" Killian asked, suddenly uncomfortable. It had occurred to him that if he did reclaim his rights as the heir, he could easily grant Mailin a life of comfort. Yet Vale had worked hard over the years to grow the

Teranos wealth. Killian wouldn't steal the fruits of his brother's labor to provide for his woman.

Mailin eased the apprehensive knot in his chest with an easy laugh and a twinkle in her eyes. "Heavens, no. What I want is to be yours. You can be anything . . . bondsman, farmer, or mighty lord, and I'll be happy to be yours."

"Even if I were a penniless ne'er do well?" he asked with a teasing grin.

"You could be as broke as a sewer rat, and I'd still be yours," she declared with a haughty tilt of her chin. "Besides, we won't ever starve. I have skill enough to care for the both of us."

He tapped her nose. "That you do," he agreed. But he would be damned if he'd lead a life where he contributed nothing to their hearth. More, how could he protect her properly if he didn't have access to the full breadth of his mageborn powers? Protecting her from convicts with their psychic abilities stripped was one matter, but in a realm where they'd inevitably encounter mages of all manner of psychic strength? Killian wouldn't stand a chance against a telekinetic. Now Mailin was *his*, compromising her safety was not an option.

She must have read his thoughts, for worry clouded her gaze. "Please, Killian. Let's just leave while we have the chance. I don't like the idea of you confronting Vale." She reached for his hand. "There is a man in Batuhan. One they call the Curator. Rumors say he is a halfbreed with unique powers. He may be able to help us disappear."

Killian flattened his lips with a firm shake of his head, glad he'd come to his senses before he'd inadvertently sent Mailin to the doorstep of this . . . Curator. Whoever and whatever the man was, he sounded like a halfbreed with Unseelie blood. Unlike the Seelie, the dark fae were always implicated in trouble. Even if Killian and Mailin did manage to disappear in some backwater town, Vale would never stop hunting them. Killian's brother was not a man to forgive; neither was he a man to forget. A confrontation with Vale was unavoidable. Unless . . .

"I could appeal to the Echelon. An archmage has the power to void a blooded bond."

Mailin widened her eyes and shuddered. "That's even worse! Don't even think about it. Archmages do not grant favors. Even if they did agree to it, they wouldn't do it without taking something in return."

Killian nodded his agreement. "I knew one once. Lord Archmage Declan Thorne. He went by a different name then, but he served in the enclave as a boy."

Mailin's eyes rounded. "The archmage served at the enclave? What was he like?"

"Not the friendly sort. He kept mostly to himself." Then again, all the boys did. The enclave was not a place conducive to friendships. "Cold. Almost apathetic."

Hence confronting Vale was likely his best option.

Yet Mailin held fast to her reservations. "Killian, what if he disagrees? Have you forgotten how he drove a dagger into your gut? He's ruthless, to say the least."

He exhaled. "Vale *is* ruthless, but he isn't unreasonable. If he truly wanted me dead, he would have killed me in my sleep a long time ago." He gave an absent tug at the collar around his neck. His brother could easily impose his will and constrict the collar. Choke him into submission, or death. But Vale had done neither. His little brother might not admit it, but he was attached to Killian for the same reason Killian had enabled his maltreatment. They were brothers, and had been close once, no matter the sins that had driven them apart.

"Give me a chance, Mailin. If I fail, we'll do what you say." Killian pressed a kiss on her temple to soothe the unhappy curve of her lips. "One way or another, we'll be together."

It was the first promise he'd ever made to a woman—and one he had no intention of breaking.

L eaving Mailin behind was the hardest part of the journey, but Killian knew she was safest at the tavern. He walked the cobblestone path of the capital to the dusty streets leading past the outskirt towns until he arrived in the farmlands of Teramaine.

Speaking with the vicegerents had been a task simpler than he'd imagined. He'd made his way to Teramaine's three major villages—all of which he had regular dealings with—and the moment he made his wishes known, the officials had been quick to offer their support.

"I still remember the day your father first brought you here. You were nothing but a squalling infant, and Railea bless the man's soul, he was so proud. Even with Lord Vale claiming the lordship, we remember you. You've always treated us with respect, and for that, you will always have our loyalty," declared one vicegerent. The other two had echoed the same sentiments.

Feeling sorely humbled, Killian made his way toward the Teranos Estate. For all the years he'd chosen to hide, his people hadn't forsaken him.

Autumn was fast approaching, and tall rows of golden corn stretched in every direction. The wind whistled through the sheaves as though welcoming him home. Yet the closer he was to the estate, the heavier his heart grew. Would this be the last time he ever walked through these fields? As a child, he'd thought Teramaine would be his to tend and manage—now it never would. Yet, he loved it all the same. His chest expanded as he breathed in the sweet fragrance of corn nearly ripe in its husk.

Almost as sweet as the soft, honeyed fragrance of Mailin.

A grin split his face at the thought of her waiting for him back at the tavern. She had made a fanatic out of him, the soul-stirring temptress with her tender touches and lusty kisses.

Never had he wanted a woman with such reckless zest, only to be welcomed with such wanton zeal. She might have spent most the night beneath him, but it felt as though she'd lifted rocks from his shoulders.

He might never fully atone for his sins, but she had given him a taste of what life could be, and he wanted so desperately to *live*.

The Teranos Estate grew in the horizon from a speck of beige to a stately mansion of smooth walls and white pillars. Grandiose. Imposing. A home that hadn't been his since the day he'd left for the enclave.

Killian snuck in through the servants' quarters. Avoiding his brother's office and favorite lounges, he made his way up the four flights of stairs to his sleeping chamber. Vale couldn't seem to stand to see him dwell amongst the servants, but Killian's little brother made it clear Killian no longer belonged in the family home by relegating him to the attic. An arrangement which suited him well. He enjoyed the privacy.

He pushed away a crate he used as a bedside table to reveal a loosened floorboard. Pulling the lacquered board up, Killian fished out a pouch. Tested its weight. Heavy enough. He tucked it into his pants' pocket.

Then Killian went for Vale. He found his brother by instinct.

Vale was a creature of habit. On the days he wasn't whoring, he spent most of his time around the stable grounds, breaking in his stallions and riding his geldings.

Vale was perched atop a magnificent stallion when Killian

arrived. There was not a hint of surprise on his brother's expression. "Scar," he said, his tone clipped. "And where is my recalcitrant bride?"

Killian blinked, startled by his brother's nonchalance. Apprehension twisted his gut. He hadn't planned on Vale's knowledge. "Commander Darragh already paid you a visit, then?"

"Indeed." Vale urged his horse closer and peered down the length of his nose. "Dar arrived last night to deliver the news himself, fearing my bride-to-be was now despoiled, given the two days she spent on that island filled with such dirty, decrepit souls."

Killian scowled. "Mailin was not compromised on that island."

She was compromised in a tavern.

Vale sat high on his horse, his spine straight as he studied Killian with a disquieting calm. "Took *good* care of my bride, did you?"

Killian grimaced, unable to conjure the words he had planned to say. He wouldn't make excuses, for he wasn't sorry. Neither could he bring himself to lie, not to his own brother . . . and from the look in the other man's eyes, Vale knew it.

The psychic punch hit him square in his chest, emptying his lungs and sending him to his knees. Killian took the next punch without attempting to avoid it.

"Vale," he gasped. "Listen to me—"

"How dare you touch what is mine?" Another wallop from an invisible source sent Killian sprawling with the taste of iron coating his mouth.

Vale alighted from his perch with easy grace, his boots stomping onto the dirt inches from Killian's face. "She belongs to me!"

Killian spat the blood pooling in his mouth. "You don't even love her!"

Mailin was no more precious to Vale than a prized trophy to be paraded in court.

"Love?" Vale sneered as he grabbed fistfuls of Killian's shirtfront and hauled him up. "Is that what you are? *In love*? With a halfbreed I paid twenty thousand jaroobis for?"

"I will repay the sum. I will—"

"And how will you accomplish that? You have no coin, no *name*. You are Scar, and you're alive because of my grace. And this is how you repay me?" he yelled. "By swiving *my* bride?"

Killian shoved off Vale's hold, anger boiling in his chest. "I am your brother!"

"You haven't been my brother since the moment you killed *her*!"

Vale's vicious words sliced furrows into Killian's chest, slashing through to his heart. Killian staggered back, swarmed by a familiar sense of wretchedness. Vale had adored their mother as much as he had detested their father.

"I am sorry," Killian whispered, his perpetual apology that never found purchase. "If I could turn back time, I would never have warped to Mother in that state. I never meant to hurt her. I never meant to hurt you."

Killian met his brother's furious gaze, but that was the extent of his apology. He would not apologize for taking Mailin. It was a decision he'd made consciously, with a bone-deep confidence that no man could love her the way he did.

"You no longer need me, Vale, and I can't do this anymore." He tugged at the metal around his neck, a collar he'd willingly worn for over a century. "Release me, or I'll bring this matter to the Council of Amereen."

"The council?" Vale snickered. "Are you so naïve as to believe the councilors would take your word over mine?"

Killian flattened his lips. "I have the support of a number of your vicegerents, all who are willing to testify to my identity. Release me, Vale. Let's not make a spectacle in court."

His brother's visage darkened and his fists clenched.

"*Release* you?" Vale gave a shout of laughter. "Release you so you can reclaim your position as the Teranos heir? Take my bride and everything I've ever worked for?"

"You mistake me, brother. The Teranos title and everything that goes with it is yours. I do not want it." There were only two things Killian wanted. "My freedom and your word to let Mailin go are all I want from you."

Vale scoffed. "You will get nothing from me, and neither will those straw-stuffed officials who think to go behind my back. But I will promise you this: once I retrieve my delinquent bride from the hollow where you've hidden her, I will ride her until she goes limp." A malicious curl of his lips. "And I'll do it while *you* watch."

Killian snapped his head forward with enough force to slam into Vale's nose with an audible crack. Vale yelped, but before he could retaliate, Killian rammed a fist into his brother's gut.

Vale threw a punch, but his brother had never been Killian's match when it came to fisticuffs. Killian served another blow. "Try it and I'll kill you."

Vale laughed, a flat and mirthless sound. Killian's fist halted midair as he stared at his brother's already bruising face. "You would turn against your own brother, all for the first woman who allows you between her legs?"

Killian dropped his hand, shame and frustration flushing simultaneously on his face.

"Vale," he said with a hard swallow, trying to appeal to the other man as a brother and not a bondsman. "When I'm with her, I feel peace. I feel . . . whole. I love her, Vale. You have my word that I'll repay what you've paid for her. Let me go, and you'll never need to see me again."

Vale narrowed his gaze. "You truly intend to forfeit all claim as the firstborn?"

Killian nodded and slackened his grip. "You have my word. I would never—"

The psychic punch hit him square in the face.

His collar began to heat, the metal constricting over his neck until Killian began to choke. "Vale!" He wheezed, clawing at the collar in a futile attempt to loosen its hold.

He sprawled on the floor, gasping for air, and barely felt it when Vale's booted foot landed on his midsection.

"Let this be a reminder. Killian Teranos died a long time ago. I buried him alongside my parents. You are Scar, and you will always be a bondsman. Nothing more. Just like Mailin is my chosen bride. The day I let her go is when I tire of her, and even then, she'll do well to serve my men."

Vale's bitter smirk was the last thing Killian saw before everything faded to oblivion.

SEVENTEEN

MAILIN

Humming the lullaby, Mailin studied her reflection in the mirror as she trimmed the ends of her hair to even out the choppiness she'd caused with the blade.

Upon Killian's departure, she'd felt so bereft that she'd wandered down into the tavern and charmed a pair of scissors from Saoire in an effort to keep herself occupied.

She combed her fingers through her hair with a sigh, missing the length of her locks. A delicious shiver ran down her body as she remembered a far larger hand tugging at her shortened tresses as he pinned her to the bed. Killian certainly hadn't minded the length.

Heat bloomed low in her belly as her gaze tracked the rumpled sheets of the bed behind her. Her skin prickled as though the mere thought of him had conjured his hands on her skin. *Killian.* Being parted from him was almost a physical ache.

At the thought of him seeing Vale, her stomach twisted into knots.

She couldn't quite shake the feeling of unease Killian didn't seem to share. He had been confident he could convince his brother to free him, but all she could see was Vale plunging the knife into Killian's gut as though he were worth less than an animal.

Nevertheless, Killian had made her a promise. And she trusted him. Implicitly.

Mailin shoved the anxiety from her chest and forced her focus back to her reflection. She was in the midst of braiding when the fervent knock startled her.

Frowning, Mailin opened the door to a distraught-looking Saoire.

"My lady," whispered the taverner's wife in an unusually low voice, her eyes darting with a wariness that roused alarm in Mailin's chest. "There's a man downstairs. A high mage. Claims he's looking for a woman who *belongs* to him. He's ready to tear up Rufus and my other boys for keeping him from coming up here."

The blood drained from Mailin's face, and her knees threatened to buckle.

"I must go."

Saoire grimaced. "I thought so. Come with me. There's a way to get you out the back, if you're willing to climb down the trellis." Saoire glanced at the scissors still clutched in Mailin's hands. "I'd keep those if I were you."

Mailin was under no illusion a pair of scissors would defend her against Vale, but she nodded her gratitude and slipped them into her pocket anyway. Carrying something sharp gave her a measure of comfort.

"Quickly," the matron hissed on a low breath as she beckoned. "This way."

Wordlessly, Mailin followed Saoire down the hallway, wincing at the creaking floorboards. The older woman unlocked the windows. "Here. A small jump and you'll hit the trellis."

Mailin was on the windowsill with the heat of the sweltering sun on her face when footsteps sounded on the stairwell.

Saoire's gasp caused her to still.

"I wouldn't do that if I were you," said a chillingly familiar voice. A tall, broad-shouldered figure loomed behind Saoire, his face handsome and unscarred, his features hard and utterly devoid of compassion.

He had a hand casually slung around Saoire's shoulder, but Mailin didn't need to see the terror in the matron's gaze to sense his threat.

Mailin bared her teeth in disgust. "I didn't know high mages could romp about, terrorizing citizens."

Vale laughed. He smirked at Saoire and patted her cheek as though she were a child. "Oh, I wouldn't dream of hurting her . . . *Scar*, on the other hand?" Another bark of laughter. "Jump, and I can guarantee you'll never see him again."

K illian awoke with a gasping breath.

He reached instinctively for his neck and realized he was bound. He tugged sluggishly at the metal cuff chaining his wrist. Killian frowned. He was lying on a tiled balcony attached to a stately bedchamber. *Vale's* bedchamber. His brother had chained him to the balustrade of the balcony . . . which offered a perfect view of the large bed beyond.

Sickness pooled in his gut.

I will ride her until she goes limp. And I'll do it while you watch.

"Vale!" Killian roared. Silence answered him.

He thrashed, trying to free his wrist, but all he managed was to topple the tiny, round table and its chairs. The table crashed beside him, spilling the ashtray and sending its contents into the air near his feet.

Killian twisted frantically to see the Teranos grounds below.
No gardeners. No servants. Not a soul. And even if they were
around, who would dare defy a high mage by helping a bondsman?

Killian groaned.

He should have listened to Mailin. He was a fool. He
huddled on the ground, feeling very much like the child he'd been
when first sent to the enclave, missing his mother.

He should never have agreed to his father's plans. He should
never have left the enclave. He should never have left Mailin this
morning.

He should never have thought to *reason* with Vale.

A moan leaked from his throat. Had he truly believed *he* was
the right man for Mailin? Vale was right. He was nothing but a
scarred-up brute who would never amount to anything. He'd
allowed lust to cloud his brain, and now Mailin would pay for his
foolish dreams and desires. He stared at the bed, which seemed to
taunt him with its perfectly white sheets, as he envisioned what Vale
would do to her.

Mailin . . .

He could still taste her on his tongue, hear her husky laugh
in his ears. Killian sucked in another shuddering breath as he
replayed the previous night in his mind—her writhing beneath him,
flushed with pleasure. He had given her that, hadn't he? He had
wrung moans of ecstasy from her throat. More, he had made her a
promise.

He gritted his teeth, his spine growing rigid.

He would damn well keep that promise.

His gaze darted to the round ashtray that had rolled off the
tiny sitting table. Just within his reach. With his free hand, he picked
it up. Like everything his brother owned, it was lavish, crafted from
polished marble. Killian hefted the heavy weight in his free hand as

he thought of Mailin.

Clenching his jaw, he smashed it against the knuckles of his chained hand. Pain jolted, so agonizing he nearly dropped the makeshift bludgeon. Nausea broiled up his throat as he stared at his bloodied knuckles trembling against the balustrade. Killian bit the inside of his cheek, stifling his screams as he continued to smash.

Whether or not he cared to admit it, his time in the enclave *had* taught him many skills—one of them the ability to withstand gruesome pain.

Killian didn't stop until his tongue was coated in blood and he'd shattered enough bones to squeeze his mangled hand through the shackle.

illian didn't return to the tavern.

Instead, he rode east, farther away from the capital, farther away from Mailin. He had staggered through the mansion, cradling his wounded hand and leaving a trail of blood in his wake until he'd arrived at the stables, where he'd pilfered a horse. One of Vale's prized stallions.

No one tried to stop him. Not the wide-eyed servants nor the stoic stablemaster he'd encountered along the way. Whether they did so from compassion or fear of the wildness in his appearance, Killian did not know. He was running out of time—and his destination was at least an hour's ride from the Teranos Estate.

Now that Vale knew the truth, he would hunt them down like dogs. Even if Killian managed to elope with Mailin, he would only condemn her to a lifetime of running. It would be a matter of time until his brother found them, and Killian would be powerless to defend her. As long as the collar remained around his neck, Vale would always have the upper hand.

The Castle of Amereen was a formidable sight with its dark sandstone walls and forbidding buttresses, perched at the apex of Torgerson Peaks.

Killian rode up to the castle portcullis. He'd expected the entrance to be closed, but the latticed grille was raised. A merchant trundled past the entrance in a donkey-pulled cart. Lady luck was on his side. Only sentries manned the entrance. Killian faced a gangly foot soldier, his face peppered with freckles and his hair a red lash of color against somber walls.

"I'm here to see the lord archmage Thorne." When the sentry only stared at him as though he'd requested to see the Goddess Railea herself, Killian repeated his intent. Archmages didn't take audiences with commoners.

"Tell him Killian Teranos requests an audience."

The sentry eyed the bloodied linens wrapped over Killian's mangled fist, and his brows furrowed at the collar around Killian's neck, but he straightened. "Teranos? As in the high mage Teranos?"

Killian shook his head. "*Killian* Teranos."

"What did he say, Philip?" interjected the sentry manning the other side of the portcullis.

The freckle-faced sentry, Philip, scoffed. "Fellow here thinks just because he shares the last name of Lord Teranos, he can come riding up to the castle gates, asking to see the *sire* himself." Philip's words floated far enough to reach the ears of the other guards along the length of the castle gates, inciting a rash of guffaws.

"I only need five minutes of his time," Killian insisted.

"Let me tell you something, my good man," said Philip with a chuckle as he ran a hand through his ginger hair, a grin on his youthful face. "I've worked here for thirty-odd turns of the sun now, and I've only ever glimpsed the sire in the sparring field! Even then, he was so far off I barely saw his face. Who in the five realms do you think you are to demand an audience with one of the Echelon?"

"If you'll just inform him that—" Killian faltered. What message, indeed, could the sentry carry that would catch the attention of an archmage? "Tell him an acquaintance—a *friend*— from the enclave needs his help."

"A friend?" Philip only cackled harder. "Ho, boys! This fellow here thinks to call himself—"

Every minute the blistering fool wasted was another minute of risking Mailin in Vale's hands. So Killian did the last thing he could think of to get himself an audience with an archmage—he punched Philip in the teeth.

All laughter ceased, the surrounding sentries snapping to attention.

They swarmed him, but Killian had already anticipated their reaction. Looping the reins around the forearm of his injured hand, he unsheathed his sword and kicked the stallion in the flank, urging it forward despite the clamoring guards around them. He was careful with his sword, battling only to disarm, not to maim or kill. He was fighting to garner attention, not land himself at the gallows.

He forced himself through the entrance, the stallion crossing the golden glow of the castle wards before he was dragged from his mount. Killian landed hard on the ground. Rough hands shoved his face into the dirt as they relieved him of his sword. Someone knocked into his mangled hand, eliciting a wave of searing agony. Killian howled and sent his unharmed fist in an uppercut to the sentry's jaw. The man dropped to the ground.

"*Enough!*" The single word cleaved through the air, seizing every soldier within the vicinity. "What in Railea's name is going on here?"

Killian shook himself free from the sentries' grappling hands only to meet a familiar face.

Darragh.

"Lord Commander!" Killian shouted, vying to be heard over the cacophony.

The commander narrowed his eyes as recognition struck. "*You.* What are you doing here?"

Killian dragged in a deep breath. The commander could easily help or lock him away, so Killian straightened his spine and squared his shoulders to lend more credibility to a farce that could well send him to an early grave. This was his last chance. If he couldn't fulfill the one promise he'd made to the one woman who had become his world, then he would rather not live at all.

"I'm here to see Lord Archmage Thorne. I have something to offer, something he wants."

The commander folded his arms and laughed. "What could you possibly have that is of value to an archmage?"

"Take me to him, and you'll find out."

Darragh raised a brow as he met the challenge in Killian's gaze. "And here I thought to spare your life after a good flogging"— his lips twisted into a sneer—"But who am I to deny a man his death?"

EIGHTEEN

KILLIAN

K illian was led into what must be the archmage's receiving
hall, a chamber so massive the entire Teranos mansion could
easily fit inside. Little wonder Vale adored court life. He
appreciated opulence, and this castle was steeped in it.

Arched windows allowed fresh light into the hall,
illuminating the gilded paintings and finely woven tapestries
gracing the walls.

Crystal chandeliers dripped from the fresco of a domed
ceiling, winking light across the solemn warriors sculpted into the
friezes. They seemed to glower down at him as his boots tracked dirt
over the pearlescent marble. His heart thundered to his own footfalls
as if he were a prisoner marching to a death knell.

Killian's gut clenched as he made his way toward the dais
where the archmage sat on a massive throne of gold and glass. Even
from the distance, Killian could feel the weight of the archmage's
scrutiny. A hundred years had passed, and the gangly boy had since
filled out his frame and turned into a man. A boy he had once known

as Declan Alvah now called himself Lord Archmage Thorne, his name changed to reflect the years he'd served at the Thorne Enclave. The same enclave where Killian had lost his childhood.

The archmage sat with apparent ease, yet an undercurrent of tightly restrained psychic energy rippled the air, radiating from him like heat from a bonfire.

Killian kept his head high and his shoulders squared even as he bent his knee. "Lord Archmage Thorne," he murmured. "Thank you for granting me an audience."

A flicker of lashes was the only movement the other man made as he assessed Killian with eyes of soulless green. The bastard had always been taciturn, but now he could well be as frigid as the frozen peaks of Flen.

"Commander Darragh has informed me of your claims to be . . . Killian Teranos." The archmage gave the barest tilt of his head before he said, "To my knowledge, Hendrik's firstborn died in the enclave."

Darragh, who had moved to stand guard on the first step of the curved dais, smirked.

Killian dropped both knees to the ground. "Forgive the impertinence of my claims, Lord Archmage, but I assure you, I am most certainly not dead." Killian swallowed his nervousness as the archmage clearly considered his words. He wanted to remind the archmage that they had dined on several occasions at the same table and had even scrubbed the halls together once, but he didn't dare.

Memories of the enclave were ones Killian was eager to forget, and he was *almost* certain the archmage wished for the same. The guardians of that hallowed, yet nightmarish place had to haunt every soul who'd ever had the misfortune to set foot in it—yet the archmage carried the enclave in his name.

If the archmage recognized him in any way, he gave no indication. Still, Killian had not yet been reduced to a pile of smoking ash. That had to count for something.

"You serve the high mage Vale Teranos." Silken words phrased more as an observation than a query. "Yet you come here without his sanction."

Killian bowed his head low as he sought to explain the nature of his relationship with Vale. "Yes, Lord Archmage, but I—"

"What is it you have that you believe I want?" The archmage wore no readable expression, but Darragh and the soldiers flanking the dais wore open smirks, as though they expected Killian to meet death at any moment.

Killian swallowed again. "I apologize for making such an insinuation—"

"Do not waste my time, Killian Teranos." Words that could well be a silent whip.

He should never have made such a bold claim, but piquing Darragh's interest was the only way he could gain an audience.

Killian lifted his chin. "Loyalty, Lord Archmage."

The archmage lifted a single brow in response while quiet snickers filled the room.

"Loyalty?" Darragh repeated with a scoff. "You forced your way through the gates and demanded an audience with the sire to offer *loyalty*?" An incredulous laugh. "You witless sod, every man and woman in Amereen owe the sire fealty."

Killian refused to lower his gaze. If he died in the next instant, he didn't want to die with his head bowed. "It is true every citizen in Amereen owes you fealty, Lord Archmage, but how many offer true loyalty?"

A moment passed, and still he breathed. Emboldened, Killian gestured to the collar around his neck. "I seek freedom from Vale Teranos's service. I know you have the power to undo a blooded bond, my lord. My liege. In exchange, you will have my deepest gratitude, and with that, my unending loyalty. For as long as

I live."

He was effectively selling his soul to the devil, but if there was a chance to be free from the collar binding his powers, Killian would take it.

The archmage shifted in his seat. "You believe I would annul your bond and override your contract with Lord Teranos for the simple loyalty of a bondsman?"

Killian's heart sank. When the archmage put it that way, his request sounded obnoxious at best.

"How can you offer me loyalty, when you are intent on betraying the man you're bound to serve?" The archmage lifted a hand, and two guards dragged Killian to his feet, hauling him away.

"It is true I wear Vale's collar, but I owe him no bond," Killian protested. The guards exerted more force, so Killian rammed a knee into one's gut to free himself.

"How dare you," Darragh said with a snarl. "Have him flogged and thrown into the dungeons."

"No! I do not owe Vale anything. I am his brother! I am the firstborn of Teranos—you must know this. You knew me!"

"Forgive me for bringing this fool to your feet, my liege." Darragh gave a low bow before he warped and rematerialized directly before Killian. The commander's fist connected smoothly with Killian's temple, and black specks erupted across his sight.

Killian thrashed against the guards' hold. He bucked with enough force to slam his head against the guard manhandling him, knocking the soldier to the ground. Darragh scowled, and an invisible fist slammed into Killian's chest, emptying his lungs and buckling his knees. More hands grabbed at him, forcing him to the ground.

"*Cease.*"

The intervention was so unexpected that all eyes stared up at the man who remained seated on the throne. A man who radiated such coldness he could well be part of the marbled friezes etched into the walls, almost too unearthly to be part of this realm, and one whose gaze currently held a flicker of . . . interest.

"You dare strike my men in my presence?"

"I wasn't done." Killian seethed before he added, "Surely you remember me? Surely—"

"It is a widely known fact that Hendrik Teranos's firstborn son *died* because he was too weak to withstand life at the enclave," countered Darragh.

Damn Vale and his lies. Though Killian had no one to blame. He had enabled his brother's aspersions.

"You used to warp from the enclave when you thought no one was looking," Killian blurted, staring up at the implacable expression of the archmage. "I noticed, but I never gave you away."

A hush descended on the hall. Killian had no way of knowing if he'd revealed a secret that would get him killed. But he'd be damned if he allowed Vale's lies to continue.

"Lord Hendrik's son was reputed to be one of considerable swordsmanship," the archmage mused, breaking the chilling silence. He tilted his head a fraction in apparent consideration. "I will offer you a deal. Defeat Darragh in combat, and I will release you from your bond to Vale."

Killian blinked.

Darragh furrowed his brows. "*Sire?*"

"You may both choose a weapon," the archmage continued, unfazed by his commander's deepening frown. "The first to draw blood will be the victor."

"And if I lose?" Killian dared ask.

The archmage issued an aloof shrug, as though he were remarking on the life of a man already dead. "Then you will be subject to whatever punishment my commander deems appropriate."

Darragh's unrestrained snicker echoed in the large chamber while the surrounding soldiers smirked. The lord commander was a renowned telekinetic with the ability to warp at will. The archmage might as well have signed Killian's death warrant.

The archmage's lips lifted in a wholly unexpected curve, a minuscule smile as unnerving as a cobra flaring its head. "Darragh will only use his physical abilities," the archmage added before reclining in his seat, a king expecting a show.

Killian expelled a bated breath. Then he went down to his knees and bowed, low enough his forehead kissed the cool marble. Barring the commander's use of psychic power made the fight *almost* fair. Darragh's leather armor meant Killian had lower chances of drawing blood, and his self-mutilated hand was a major handicap. Still, he had just been given a viable chance. He would not waste it.

He rose swiftly to his feet. The soldiers around him receded to the room's perimeter. Killian shook out his fists and grimaced as pain shot through his damaged hand. He would have to fight one-handed.

Lucky Vale hadn't thought to chain his dominant hand.

"Well, then. Let's make it quick, shall we?" Darragh said with a curl of his lips, seemingly recovered from his shock. "You've wasted enough of our time."

The commander unsheathed the double-edged broadsword strapped to his hip.

Killian's own sword had been lost in the scuffle as he barged through the castle entrance, but the archmage had promised him a weapon.

A man, clad in nonmartial robes of white, beckoned him to the wall bearing a collection of magerian weaponry. Lances, battleaxes, broadswords . . . Killian selected his favored weapon. He hefted the double-handed longsword, the warrior in him relishing the feel of a fine magerian blade. The pommel was a good weight and the metal shone with a wicked glint. He made a practice swing before he turned to the commander, who had already assumed a combative posture.

Holding his damaged hand to his back, Killian took a deep breath and willed his mind to focus. He had barely shifted in his stance before Darragh came at him like an arc of lightning—swift, strong, and unforgiving.

Steel kissed steel, the sharpened edges singing against one another in a lethal symphony. With single-minded determination, Killian matched every blow and dodged every attack. His skill had only been honed over the years as Vale regularly made him deal with bandits or highwaymen who thought to impose upon Teramaine lands. Somehow he managed to gain ground on his advances until he had Darragh nearly backed into the line of observing soldiers.

Then the commander smirked. And Killian realized he'd been played.

Darragh had been drawing out the fight like a cat toying with its prey, tiring Killian's strength and testing his skills. Killian pivoted to dodge a well-aimed thrust of the commander's sword. A balled fist careened into his face, the metal panes on the commander's gauntlet connecting with his cheekbone in a dizzying crunch. His head snapped back.

Killian backstepped, nearly losing his balance in an effort to evade the slashing tip of the commander's sword. A single break of his skin and he would condemn Mailin to a lifetime pinned beneath his brother's thumb—and more.

At the thought of Mailin claimed by another man, a roar of fury worked its way from his throat. Rage renewed his vigor and desperation turned him into a demon.

Like a man possessed, he parried Darragh's merciless blows and feinted a thrust. The commander sidestepped, but he didn't guard his head. Killian's elbow collided with his face. Darragh staggered, shock coloring his eyes, *blood* trickling from the corners of his mouth.

Before Killian could shout his triumph, an invisible force emptied his lungs.

He stumbled to the ground, gasping for breath. The taste of iron filled his mouth. He swiveled. Rolled. A fraction slower and Darragh's sword would have impaled his chest. The commander was no longer fighting to draw blood. He was fighting to kill.

Killian vaulted up, his booted feet connecting with Darragh's chin. The commander fell to his back. Before his opponent could pick himself up, Killian angled the tip of his sword at his throat.

"Do it." The command came from the dais, words spoken with such soft intensity that Killian paused warily. "You have earned the right."

Killian stared up at the archmage before returning his gaze to the commander, whose eyes were wildly dilated. He raised his sword high.

And brought it down.

Instead of embedding the sword in the commander's neck— which would most definitely be fatal—he plunged it into the mage's gut. The commander would live under a healer's touch.

Darragh writhed, blood gurgling from his throat.

Killian turned toward the dais. "Lord Archmage, I—"

He widened his eyes when the archmage disappeared from the throne only to materialize before them. The teleport was so smooth it happened within the span of a single second. Glacial green eyes bored down on his for one instant before the archmage turned to wrench the sword from Darragh's gut.

"A man who cheats is not fit to lead my army," the archmage said as though he were making a mundane comment about the weather before he brought the sword down in one swift motion. The commander didn't get a chance to scream before his head was rolling in a puddle of blood.

Shocked silence suffused the chamber. The archmage tossed the sword beside Darragh's body, and the clang of steel on marble rang like a thunderclap.

Killian stared, every hair on his body standing on end. The archmage, tall and unruffled beside the body of his decapitated commander, was a sight more chilling than the grotesquerie of the severed head staring sightlessly up at the frescoed ceiling.

"Will you grant me my freedom?" Killian dared ask as the archmage stepped back from the widening pool of blood seeping from Darragh's body.

"No."

Belligerence burned in Killian's throat, stoking his boldness. "I thought you were a man of your word."

"You just cost me a commander. The deal is void."

Killian sputtered. "*You* killed him."

"He was a dead man the moment he chose to defy my orders." The archmage turned and met Killian's gaze with unnerving intensity. "You are weak, Killian Teranos. You gave mercy where mercy was unjustified. For that, you deserve no reprieve. Now get out of my sight before I change my mind and kill you for causing a disturbance in my court."

Perhaps it was the adrenaline still coursing in his veins, or perhaps death no longer looked so daunting since he'd all but damned himself.

"You are no different from Darragh!" Killian yelled after the archmage's turned back. "If he was a cheat, then you are a fucking liar!"

The retaliation came so quickly that Killian was lying on the ground and the archmage hadn't even lifted a finger. Soldiers pinned him down, swords bristling at his neck. "Insolent vermin!" snarled one soldier.

"Shall we rip out his tongue, sire?" jeered another.

Killian gave a bark of hysterical laughter. "Damn you, Archmage! Fight me if you dare! I'll show you how I feel about mercy!"

The swords lifted from his sight. Killian braced himself, yet steel did not slash his skin or stab his flesh. He staggered up to see the archmage looming over him, wearing an expression more severe than the god of death himself.

"You dare challenge *me*?"

Killian spat at the archmage's polished boots, childishly pleased to tarnish a small part of the immaculate asshole.

"If it were a fair fight, I'd wipe the floor with your silk-covered ass," he said with a reckless sneer. He was so close to death he could almost taste the edge of its scythe.

The archmage surprised him by lowering himself to his haunches so they stared eye to eye. "But life is never fair, is it?" Words so soft Killian wondered if he was meant to hear them.

The archmage rose to his feet. "You amuse me, Killian Teranos," he said, though his expression revealed not a hint of amusement. "I will give you your fight."

The bastard didn't even need to look, but the sword still glistening with Darragh's blood levitated off the ground. The end of the pommel floated smoothly into the palm of Killian's uninjured hand.

"If you draw my blood before you fall, I will annul your bond to Vale."

Before I fall. Killian laughed. He was so worn he was one step away from the eternal sleep of the damned. The archmage would have him on his back in a second.

But life is never fair, is it? The archmage's words danced in his mind, mocking his determination, taunting his resolve for freedom.

"You will honor your words this time?" Killian rasped. "If I win, you will grant me freedom?"

"Freedom from Vale," the archmage agreed with a nod, but his gaze grew shrewd. "But you will serve *me*."

"What need would an archmage have of a bondsman?" Killian demanded, unsuccessful in his attempt to hide his contempt at what must be another trick.

"I have no need for indentured servants, but I do require a replacement." The archmage gestured to Darragh's headless body on the ground and lifted his dark brows. "Preferably someone with unending gratitude and undying loyalty."

Killian blinked, dumbfounded.

The archmage rolled up his shirtsleeves, revealing muscle-corded arms etched with otherworldly symbols simmering a faint gold. He held up an open palm and did something Killian had never thought possible: a double-edged sword *manifested* in his hand in a flash of gold.

Fuck.

Killian shut his eyes and tightened his grip on the pommel of the sword in his hands. For Mailin.

With a roar, he lunged.

NINETEEN

MAILIN

The sun perched high and punishing in the cloudless skies. Sweat licked Mailin's skin, causing the fabric of her dress to cling uncomfortably as she trudged, but that was the least of her troubles.

She had never realized how unforgiving humble dirt roads could be until she'd lost a shoe over a league ago. Another sharp pebble bit into the sole of her bare foot, wrenching a stream of profanity from her lips.

"My, my, I never would have guessed what a vulgar mouth you have. Though it shouldn't surprise me, given the cuckolding whore you turned out to be." From the saddle of his mount, Vale shot an infuriating smirk over his shoulder before he spurred his stallion into a canter.

The rope tying her hands together bit into her chafed skin as she stumbled. Gritting her teeth, Mailin hastened to regain her footing lest she be dragged along the uneven road by her bound wrists—but that fate seemed forthcoming.

Her blistered and bleeding foot aside, both her legs trembled and threatened to buckle from exhaustion. Vale had leashed her to his horse with a length of rope and dragged her through the capital streets like a farmer herding swine into a slaughterhouse. His way of humiliating her, no doubt. Vale had silenced any protests from sympathetic onlookers with a single glare. No one dared challenge a high mage, not even the patrolling guards who had passed them by with their gazes averted.

"Slow down," Mailin pleaded between labored breaths. They had long left the capital behind, stuccoed shopfronts replaced by sprawling farmhouses. Rows and rows of corn spread out on either side of the dirt path, cordoning the road, silent sentries swaying in the wind. "I promise I won't run from you."

Even if Vale wasn't dragging her behind his horse, Mailin would have gone willingly to the Teranos Estate. She wouldn't—*couldn't*—run, not while Killian was subdued.

Another sharp tug of the rope caused her to stagger. "Do you take me for a fool? After all your shenanigans, you're lucky I care enough to bring you *home*, my darling bride."

"Please," Mailin said with a scathing laugh. "I'm no more a bride to you than a prized broodmare!"

"Test me again, Mailin, and I'll blister your hide before I show you exactly how a broodmare is bred," Vale said with enough threat in his tone to silence all snark from her lips. "That scarred simpleton can't possibly know what to do with a woman." His lewd laugh accompanied another over-the-shoulder smirk. "Not to worry, my dear. Soon, you'll learn what it is to be with a real man, and Scar will learn never to touch what doesn't belong to him."

Sickness swarmed in her gut like a locust plague. "What have you done to him?" she asked for what must have been the hundredth time. "What have you done to Killian?"

"Killian?" he mused. "Gave you his name, did he?"

Mailin clamped her lips shut, unnerved by the depth of bitter resentment in his tone.

"When I'm through with him, he'll cut out his own tongue before he uses the name again."

Indignation made her reckless. "He's your *brother*! He never meant for any of it to happen. Can't you see he's been mourning the death of your parents as long as you have?"

The horse nickered and came to such an abrupt halt Mailin nearly fell to her knees. Vale alighted from the saddle and stalked closer to loom over her.

He grasped her chin so she had no choice but to look up to his face. "Revealed the family tragedy, too, did he?" he asked. "And I suppose you think that makes him . . . what? A tortured hero of sorts?" Vale cupped the length of her jaw, his long fingers digging into her cheeks with callous intent. "Is that how he got you to spread your legs, hmm? By appealing to your romantic notions?"

Mailin shook her head to pull away from his hold, but he only tightened his grip. "Let me tell you something, my sweet, gullible bride. Scar is nothing but a softhearted fool who believes in redemption and repentance in a world where only the strong survive. That's why the dumb brute is on a leash, while I take his place as the Teranos heir."

"Your parents must be twisting in their graves," Mailin said, inching her bound hands toward the deep pocket sewn into her skirts.

"I doubt that." Vale laughed. "They parented us the way sharks do their pups. Father was a power-hungry tyrant, and Mother was willingly blind to what he was doing to her own sons. Scar might not think so, but he was the *lucky* one. Lucky he was gifted enough to be sent to the enclave, so far from home."

Mailin expelled a soft breath, her fingers closing around smooth metal. "Are you blind to the hell the guardians put him through?"

"His wounds are skin deep." Vale released her chin to caress her cheek. "Some wounds run deeper than the surface, especially the ones inflicted upon children."

In that one instant, she glimpsed such pain lurking in the depths of Vale's gaze that her heart constricted. "What did they do to you?"

Vale leaned forward. The odor of spirits and tobacco laced his breath. "They made me strong. Strong in ways Scar never will be . . . that is why I have never mourned their deaths. That is why I'll not hesitate to chain my own brother to the wall and carve fresh scars into his skin if that's what it takes to keep him in line."

Any sympathy that had stirred for him vanished, replaced by razor-edged rage. Her fingers tightened around the steel handles of the scissors she'd slipped into her pocket back at the tavern.

"You're a monster."

He smirked. "A monster *you* sought to wed."

"A mistake, but not one I regret." If she had never propositioned Vale, she would never have met Killian. When he frowned, she struck so swiftly he didn't have a chance to flinch.

The sharp end of the scissors stabbed him deep at the fleshiest part of his pectoral. He howled in shock. Hopefully the wound would be deep enough to stall his ability to use telekinesis while his energies went to healing. A stab to the jugular would have been more certain, but . . . she couldn't kill Killian's brother.

"Stupid bitch!" He retaliated with a slap, but Mailin had anticipated that. She wrenched the scissors from his chest, her only means to slice through her bindings. She hadn't, however, accounted for the spooked horse.

Startled by its master's sudden shout, it reared and bolted, hauling Mailin along as though she were no more than a straw puppet tied to its reins. Pain erupted as the bindings around her wrists tightened and her body hauled across uneven ground.

The horse dragged her for what felt like a league down the road before finally, mercifully, coming to a whickering stop. Dazed, Mailin lay slumped. Agony streaked through joints, tearing tiny whimpers from her lips.

"Prince, get back here, you stupid horse!"

Vale's voice nudged her alert. She pushed up from the ground, muscles trembling and motions jerky as though her bones were hollow. Her palms were slick with blood—the sharpened edges of the scissors had been between her bound fingers before the horse bolted, and they had sliced deep into her palm.

Time trickled with every ragged breath whistling through her lungs. Mailin worked sluggishly to cut her bindings with the bloodied scissors while Vale advanced.

Her bindings snapped free.

Like a mouse sprung from a trap, she fled into the cornfield.

"Mailin!" Vale hollered. "Don't you dare run from me!"

She tore through the field, batting past leafy stalks and protruding husks, weaving through the tall rows in a desperate attempt to hide from her captor. She ran until her heart threatened to burst from her chest and slowed to catch her breath.

Bad idea.

Claustrophobia caught up to compound the fear simmering in her veins. She was completely closeted by sheaves and sheaves of corn, with no sense of where she was. A mocking breeze whistled past, swaying stems and rustling leaves. A noise sounded close, and she whirled, half expecting to see Vale's cruel smirk between the waving corn. Nothing.

She stilled, no longer certain which way was ahead.

More rustling sounded to her left.

No one emerged. It was only her imagination. Had Vale relented? She had wounded him, and while not fatal for a mage, a stab in the chest was no superficial injury. Her pulse began to slow when a low snarl sounded so close that ice snaked through her veins.

"Here now, little dove. You can't hide from me."

Killian whipped forward, but the archmage pivoted and spun, deflecting his advances with the grace of a battle-seasoned swordmaster. Clearly, the man was not a king who had grown soft from the silk and satin of court life, nor was he an archmage who relied solely upon his psychic prowess.

Killian launched another attack, which the archmage smoothly evaded.

The more aggressive his assault, the less the archmage seemed to engage—a deft dodge, a spry sidestep, a nimble jump. Like an indolent cat twitching its tail to flick off an annoying fly, he expended minimal energy with his every action, parrying only to prevent Killian from drawing blood without making advances of his own. And he did it all with a hand clasped behind his back.

The archmage mimicked his handicap. Not out of honor, but rather, a form of subtle humiliation.

He wasn't even giving Killian a proper fight. He was merely drawing him to exhaustion.

Bastard.

Killian bared his teeth. He would carve that immaculate expression right off the archmage's face if that was what it took. He drew back and circled his opponent, his own labored breaths loud in his ears.

The archmage rolled his shoulders, his regal posture seemingly relaxed, belying the lethal undercurrent of energy that shrouded him like a dense fog. "Had enough, bondsman?"

There was no inflection in the archmage's tone, but Killian

knew a goad when he heard one. And there was enough pride left in his chest to lift his chin. "I haven't fallen yet."

A small shrug. "A matter of time."

Killian gritted his teeth. The bastard was right. With every passing second, the noose of weariness tightened around his neck. Adrenaline surging his veins was the only reason he was still upright. That, and his promise to Mailin.

Killian rolled onto the balls of his feet but leashed his instinct to charge. So far, his furious attempts to score a strike against the archmage had been akin to a blind man plunging a sword into a river hoping to spear a fish.

If he were to win his freedom, he needed to keep his wits.

Killian's gaze flicked to the series of marble columns lining the great hall. He narrowed his eyes. A fish was much easier to spear when trapped in shallow waters.

Killian didn't waste his breath with a retort. He angled his sword and lunged, his strikes strategized to steer his opponent backward. He pressed his advantage, playing upon the archmage's elusiveness until the other man was exactly where he wanted—cornered between twin columns.

The archmage's eyes flared. Then he struck.

Killian bounded back, narrowly avoiding the lethal thrust of the archmage's glowing sword point. A stinging sensation ripped up his thigh. Warmth seeped down his leg.

Bastard was not only fast. When engaged, he was alarmingly fluid. Where Darragh had been a cyclone with his sword, the archmage was a deadly riptide. A lethal undercurrent that caused nary a silent ripple across the surface of the water, only to strike at the most unpredictable times.

In four sparse moves, he wended out of Killian's reach, driving their combat back into the center of the great hall—without a single scratch on his skin.

Killian growled.

If he weren't already bloodied and battered, he would have appreciated the thrill of fighting such a stately opponent. But he was, and he didn't have the time—or energy—to spare. Killian sent his sword sailing through the air like a javelin, angled and aimed with deadly intent. The archmage reacted exactly as he hoped. He batted Killian's sword to the side, sending the weapon ricocheting into one of the glass cases tucked between marble columns, shattering glass and priceless artefacts.

The archmage raised a brow.

Killian had lost his sword, and the archmage thought him foolish.

Do or die.

With one fist swinging, Killian charged his opponent. The archmage offered no mercy. Pain struck Killian like a thunderbolt as the sword drove clean through his gut. Killian jolted, but he didn't falter. Despite driving the blade deeper, Killian used the momentum of his charge to tackle and slam the archmage onto the ground.

Killian was shuddering when the archmage shoved him off like a sack of grain.

"Keep your word," Killian croaked, trying to form audible words against the blood welling up his throat.

The archmage frowned. Slowly, he touched his cheek. A line of red welled where a glass shard had scored his skin, marring that immaculate face. Dark brows slashed as he stared at his fingertips. An unanticipated quirk hooked the side of his lips in an infinitesimal smile.

"You'll soon draw your last breath, Killian Teranos. What good will freedom do you?"

Killian had calculated his odds, or so he thought. The archmage's sword hadn't ruptured his vital organs. In theory, his wound need not be fatal if given a healer's care. Free from the collar's stifling effects, Killian had intended to warp to Mailin. But he hadn't expected the heaviness of his eyelids or the numbness stealing into his limbs.

He shook his head, refusing to give in to the beckoning lull of unconsciousness. "Keep. Your. Word," he repeated in a gurgling rasp. It was a demand of the archmage as much as it was of *himself.* He had made a promise to Mailin, and he would fight with everything he had to keep it. Down to his last breath.

The archmage crouched down. Though his expression remained stoic, there was an unmistakable flare of approval—*respect?*—in his gaze. "Granted."

Killian had always believed he had an intimate relationship with pain, believed he'd suffered enough to have robbed him of his screams. Until warm fingers clamped over his throat and the collar around his neck heated into a blistering band. His blood coagulated to ice as fire seemed to constrict his neck, the conflicting sensations melding together to chase down his limbs and up his head, infiltrating every muscle and nerve ending in his body.

He screamed.

TWENTY

MAILIN

Biting down on her lips, Mailin darted in the opposite direction from Vale's voice.

"You're only making this worse for yourself, you know," he called, as though he heard her movements.

She was making too much noise pushing through the stalks. So she stopped and waited. A long, troubling pause passed.

"Mailin . . ."

His voice had grown louder, as though he were *closer*. How was he even tracking her? Vale was no telepath; he couldn't sense her presence on the psychic plane.

"Mailin . . . where are you?"

She moved, stealthier this time, weaving through the rows, brushing past wiry stalks. Then she realized her blunder. She'd inadvertently left Vale a trail. Blood seeped from her wounded hand, staining all she touched, occasionally dripping to stain the bone-dry dirt.

Cursing herself silently, Mailin gathered the hem of her

skirts and wound them over her palm. She ran. Directly into the shadowed figure that appeared abruptly in her path, seemingly out of thin air.

She skidded to a halt, but he lunged for her.

A heavy hand clamped over her mouth, stifling her scream. She grappled to free herself, struggling wildly before she caught a whiff of his scent.

Shock stilled her.

Was she hallucinating? So desperate she'd conjured sanctuary? But he *felt* so real. Muscular arms wrapped protectively around her, his large and lithe frame—so achingly familiar—pressed against her body, solid and warm.

Safe.

"Killian?" she whispered.

Shhh, Mailin. I have you. I have you.

Relief came so swiftly Mailin sagged into his embrace. She buried her face in his chest to smother her uncontrollable sobs, her fingers scrunching into the fabric of his shirt, clinging to him as though he were a buoy in a roiling sea.

Stop crying, my love. You're safe now . . . I have you. I won't let him hurt you. I won't let anyone hurt you again.

She frowned. His voice was a deep rumble that stroked her like silk, yet something was subtly different. She glanced up in shock. She heard him, yet he hadn't spoken. Not aloud.

Then she truly *saw* him.

His face was bruised, his lower lip split, and the unscarred side of his cheek bleeding from a devastating gash. She gasped and pushed away to study the rest of him. His clothes were splattered with a sickening red, and his left arm . . . it was trembling beneath the wad of linen that bundled his hand from the wrist down.

"What did Vale do to you?" Mailin asked.

Railea's blood! His curse rolled into her mind before he

emitted an audible growl, his gaze tracking the grazes on her arms
and the gash on her palm.

"What has he done to *you*?" he asked aloud. Unconcealed
violence edged his tone, but his touch held deliberate tenderness.

Mailin couldn't seem to form coherent words, her own gaze
affixed to the strong column of his throat. Free. The metal collar was
gone. Replaced by welted, raw skin, as though the collar had been
somehow melted off.

"How?" she managed.

"I tracked you telepathically," he muttered, mistaking her
question. "Now, tell me, love, what has he done?" He cupped the
back of her head, staring at her as though he could see her thoughts.
Could he? She had never met a telepath who communicated with
such startling clarity that his voice rang clear in her mind.

She shook her head. "How did you get *free*?"

Footsteps sounded at her back. "How the fuck did you get
here?"

Killian had anticipated his brother's arrival—he could hardly
miss Vale's prowling presence on the psychic plane. The
moment the archmage had rid him of the collar, Killian had
been assailed by so much mental input he was almost ready to rip
off his own head.

Voices filled his mind in a ceaseless thrum, too distorted for
him to make out clear words. He was also physically exhausted, his
muscles threatening to falter.

The archmage had all but ripped the collar off with no care
for the agony he inflicted. Killian had been a step from death's door,
but the archmage had commanded one of the castle healers to his
aid. Killian did not understand the other man's show of sudden

benevolence, but neither did he question his fortune. The moment he was healed enough to stand without swaying, Killian had warped.

"How in the five hells did you escape?" Vale demanded. With a hand pressed over the bloodied patch on his chest, Vale stared at Killian's bare throat and his jaw grew slack. "Impossible . . ."

Beside Killian, Mailin's fingers tightened over his tunic. He gave her a gentle squeeze of reassurance and moved past her. Had Vale caused her more harm, Killian would have a hard time attempting this conversation. As it was, he pulled out the small pouch from the pocket of his pants, his uninjured hand trembling with uncontrollable tremors. He tossed the leather pouch at Vale, and it landed near his brother's boots, gold pieces spilling out to wink at the sun.

"That will make up for twenty thousand jaroobis and more. I want the betrothal papers burned. Mailin is no longer beholden to you."

Vale released an incredulous laugh, moving close enough to meet Killian eye to eye. "Did you rob someone to pay me for the whore?"

"She is no whore, and these are my savings." Though Killian no longer had access to his inheritance, he had secreted away gold pieces where he could over the years. He'd always yearned to leave Teramaine, but he could never seem to walk away from his brother. Now he was glad he hadn't.

"Savings?" Vale sneered. "You mean money you stole from me? I'd never expected you to stoop so low . . . all for one little bitch."

Killian clenched his teeth. Every coin in that pouch he'd damned well earned. But he didn't bother explaining. He didn't want to fight Vale. No matter his anger, he couldn't see past the boy his brother had once been. A boy Killian had watched grow into a man.

His only brother.

He issued a threat instead. "Insult her again and I swear to Railea I'll rip out your tongue."

Vale narrowed his eyes, but he must have heard the vehemence in Killian's tone for he didn't attempt another provocation. Instead, his gaze fell over Killian's bare throat.

"How did you do it?"

"Does it matter?" Killian heaved out a breath. "I don't owe you anything, Vale, and now, neither does she. From this day forward, you hold no claim on either of us."

Laughter was the last thing he expected from Vale, but his brother chortled as though he'd made a particularly humorous jest.

An invisible force slammed into Killian, buckling his knees. Dimly, he heard Mailin's shout, but Vale was already upon him, ostensibly too enraged to use anything but his fists.

"Stop it!" Killian tried to hold Vale at arm's length, but he was just so tired. "Stop this, Vale!"

Like a spiteful child, Vale snarled and threw another punch.

Enough! Killian struck out with his mind with whatever energy he had left. Vale lurched off him and sailed through the air to land in a crumpled heap over crushed corn stalks.

Not bothering to walk, Killian warped, reappearing over Vale's prone form. He wrapped a hand over his brother's throat. "Don't push me again."

Vale didn't attempt to struggle. Without the collar, they both knew he was no match for Killian in terms of martial ability. Vale shut his eyes and chuckled.

"Do it, then," he taunted.

In his periphery, Killian sensed Mailin's presence. She laid a gentle hand over his forearm as though to stop him. Only her hand was bloodied, her forearms covered in cuts and grazes that made him seethe—all Vale's doing.

"Do it!" Vale screamed, spittle flying from the corner of his lips. "I'd rather die than cede everything to you!"

"I told you I don't want any of that!" Killian lifted Vale and slammed him back into the dirt.

"The mansion, the Teranos Estate, and this." Vale gestured wildly around them. "These dirt-infested cornfields. You don't want any of it?"

Killian released Vale as though he was a poisonous snake. In that instant, he saw Vale for who he truly was. Over a century had passed, yet Vale remained the boy he'd always been—the second son striving to outshine the first—even though the sun and moon were never meant to shine at the same time.

"No, I don't," Killian repeated. He loved Teramaine, but no one could fault Vale on the governance of their lands. "All I ever wanted was my name." But the moment the words left his mouth, he knew that was no longer true. Now that Killian was finally free from the collar, he wanted his brother to be free, too. Free from the past. Free from rexweed. "Can't we just leave the past where it belongs?"

Disbelief oozed from Vale as Killian rose to his feet, leaving his brother in the dirt. When Vale made no move to stand, Killian took a wary step back. His chest heaved from exertion. He was psychically overwhelmed and physically worn. He didn't want another fight. He couldn't take *another* fight.

Mailin made to move toward him.

Killian made the mistake of turning his back.

One moment Vale was lying on the ground, and the next he had his forearms around Killian's neck in a stranglehold, choking him to his knees.

"You're right," Vale grated the words into his ear. "I should have killed and buried you beside our parents' grave. That's where *you* belong."

Killian flailed, seeking strength to warp from his brother's choking grip, but he'd exhausted the last of his psychic reserves. He was completely burnt out. He jabbed a mangled fist into Vale's side, but anger seemed to have afforded his brother added strength.

"Let go," Killian wheezed. "You don't need to do this."

"I should have done this a long time ago!"

Killian bit out a roar, working to throw his weight back to the ground in attempt to dislodge his brother's hold when Vale's grip loosened abruptly.

Vale slumped off Killian's back and staggered to his knees. Killian swiveled to see his brother clawing at something gleaming silver at his neck, gurgling on his own blood that was trickling down his lips.

The sharp end of a pair of metal scissors protruded from his throat.

Mailin stood over him, abject horror etched on her face. She went to her knees, fumbling fingers at the bleeding wound, but Vale was gone before she could begin to heal.

Killian wrapped his arms around her.

"I . . . I . . . didn't mean to kill him," she said. "I stabbed him in the back-k . . . he didn't let you g-go so I stabbed him again . . . in the t-throat . . ."

"Shhh . . . ," Killian murmured into her hair. "Mailin, it's all right."

"I didn't mean to," she repeated. "But I couldn't watch him attack you."

"I know," he said. "I know."

He didn't blame her. He had been prepared to do it himself had Mailin not intervened. Vale would never have let them go. Either way, Vale made his choice. And for the first time, Killian realized he was not responsible for those choices.

EPILOGUE

MAILIN

S unlight filtered through the heavy branches to dapple the ground while birdsong filled the air, lightening the zealous clang of swords and the shouts of men. The cacophony of sparring soldiers mirrored the excitement in Mailin's chest.

Soldiers eyed her with open curiosity, but most offered polite nods and called out pleasantries. They were not accustomed to seeing a woman near the training field—or perhaps it was simply that she appeared a loon with a big smile plastered on her face. She could barely keep from skipping along the perimeter of the vast field.

Killian had apparently battled Darragh with a single hand . . . and won. More, he had challenged the archmage *and* survived. That alone garnered him instant deference from the soldiers, and it was evident in the way the men dipped their heads around him.

The archmage hadn't only stripped Killian's collar; he had made him the new *lord commander*, a fact that had kept Mailin awake and tossing for nights on end.

If the archmage had beheaded his previous commander with such flippant ease as described by Killian, then her lover's position was precarious to say the least. Yet whenever she raised her concerns, Killian only grinned with a confidence she didn't share.

"Don't worry, temptress. I won't give him a chance to relieve me of my head." Then he had nuzzled her in a wickedly playful manner. "How else will I kiss you?"

Despite her reservations, she couldn't find it within her to dissuade him. Not even when he returned to her fatigued each evening, slicked with sweat and sometimes covered in scrapes and bruises. No matter his exhaustion, there was a light in his eyes and a spring in his steps. Excitement laced his tone whenever he spoke of his day and the responsibilities now entrusted to him. He thrived. The life of a warrior suited him, so the castle was where they remained.

Mailin was so engrossed in her thoughts she unwittingly took a wrong path in her eagerness to get to Killian's private quarters within the castle barracks. The stately, somber building loomed in the distance, but she was lost in the middle of a decidedly mazelike garden. How did people find their way around here? She couldn't seem to find the right path to the barrack's entrance.

She rounded a corner to see a fountain in which a stone seductress played a flute, water spilling from the end of her instrument. Killian had kissed her by this very fountain on one of their evening romps. Yes, this path would lead her toward the barracks. She hastened her steps. She simply couldn't wait to tell—

"Oof!"

Mailin tripped, arms flailing as she pitched forward to land on her knees.

Swearing under her breath, she pushed off the ground to scowl at the cause. A man. A very large man with inconsiderately long legs who had parked himself beside the bushes as though to ambush her. The brute didn't even bother apologizing, focusing instead on fishing for a book that must have fallen into the fountain.

"Have you got nothing better to do than to . . ." Mailin's breath seized. Chilling green eyes glared her way. But it wasn't the anger in his gaze that set her heart pounding. It was the *glyphs* etched into his exposed forearms. The symbols and shade were identical to the ones surrounding the warden's tower.

Mailin swallowed. Hard.

The glyphs seemed to glow beneath her stare. "You've ruined it." He didn't raise his voice, but ire dripped from his words.

Mailin only gaped. "I-I . . ."

The archmage turned his attention back to the soaked book cradled in his hands like an infant. He flipped the pages with reverent care as though trying to air them. "You imbecile." His gaze seemed to scald as it landed on her face. "Who in the five blazing hells are you? What are you doing in my castle?"

Indignation flared despite her shock. The castle grounds were open to all staff. It didn't seem fair for him to fault her. He was an archmage, for the love of Railea. He should be seated on a throne, not huddled by the bushes like some creeping bandit.

She wisely kept those thoughts to herself. Instead, she said, "I'm a healer's apprentice."

Not a lie. She *had* just secured the position.

She expected a scathing retort, but to her surprise, his attention was back on the book, his brows furrowed as he attempted to part sodden pages.

"*The Adventures of the Wayfarer?*" she blurted as she spied the title on the cover.

The archmage was reading . . . a *child's* fable?

"I can replace it," she quickly added when his head snapped up. A muscle ticced in his cheek as he regarded her with one fist clenched.

"I-I'll buy you a new copy."

"It is *irreplaceable*. It . . ." His gaze wandered from her face to the pointed tip of her ear. "What manner of halfbreed are you?"

Mailin swallowed, disconcerted by the sudden query. "I carry Seelie blood, sire. From my mother's side."

To her surprise, his gaze softened. "Seelie," he murmured.

Her pulse ratcheted at the near wistful quality in his tone. Her father's words echoed in her mind. *"Any archmage would relish the chance of siring halfbreed heirs. The blood running in your veins alone makes you a novelty."*

"I am Killian's . . . the lord commander's elorin de ana," she announced, and nearly kicked herself for implicating her mate. It was no secret that archmages could claim any woman within their lands. If he wanted her, Killian could do nothing to stop him.

Thankfully, his scrutiny ended at last. His attention returned to the book cradled in his arm, which had created a wet patch against his fine, silk shirt. He gave a slight tilt of his head, as though to dismiss her. "Get out of my sight."

Relief washed over her like rain. She didn't need to be told twice. With another awkward curtsy and mumbled apology, Mailin fled as swiftly as her legs could manage to put as much distance as she could between herself and the archmage.

When she arrived at the barracks, she made her way into Killian's quarters. She pushed past the plain brass door and stopped in her tracks, her uncomfortable encounter by the fountain supplanted by the man lounging on the bed.

Killian greeted her with a wide, gorgeous grin.

Something in her stomach fluttered. "Why hello there, Lord Commander," she purred, injecting enough sultriness in her tone that the brightness in his gaze darkened to a smoldering intensity. "I didn't expect you to be back so soon."

Killian was rarely back before sundown. The archmage

might pay a fair wage, but he was no easy taskmaster. Endless patrols, combat training, tactical exercises, and the gods knew what else was required of a commander of battlemages.

Her mate licked his lips. "I rescheduled so I could come home early to meet my elorin de ana."

Mailin beamed at his use of the endearment. Elorin de ana. His mate. Every time he used those words, a thrill kindled in her blood. Absently, her hands brushed the spot over her breast where his mating mark—shaped like a conch shell—had manifested on her skin the moment they established their mating bond. Their psyches were now permanently linked, their souls intertwined. If he was claimed by death, she would literally follow him to the gates of hell. She would not have it any other way.

"So, don't keep me in suspense." Killian's gaze tracked her across the room. "How did it go?"

"I got it!" Mailin rolled on the balls of her feet with a squeal. Killian pushed from the bed just as she barreled into his arms. "The healer agreed to take me as an apprentice!"

His laugh boomed in her ear as he squeezed her to his chest. "Congratulations, elorin de ana. Tell me everything."

Mailin relayed her day, including her encounter with the archmage.

Killian was snickering by the time she was done. "*The Adventures of the Wayfarer*? Are you certain?"

At her vehement nod, he gave another chortle. She gave him a playful smack, and he sobered. "Whatever it is, the book must have meant something to him. You must be more careful in the future, my elorin, and keep out of his way where possible."

Sighing, Mailin moved to curl herself against his chest, seeking the steady rhythm of his heart. He pulled away from her, backtracking to the bed to reveal a wrapped package, hidden behind the pillows.

Mailin gasped, unable to keep the delight from her voice. "For me?"

He chuckled and pushed the oversized package into her arms. "Open it."

Beaming up at him, she shook his gift. Whatever the brown paper contained felt dense but soft. She ripped off the wrapping with the finesse of an overenthusiastic child as he watched with equal eagerness.

Mailin blinked. She shook out the vividly colored fabric. Her breath shortened. The koshiyin was a midnight black, embroidered with red. The grenadi was the richest of silks, brocaded with stylized swans. She ran her fingers over the delicate motifs of widespread wings and sucked in a breath. Scarlet swans, wings stretched in flight, were woven throughout the bodice, swooping toward the flowing skirts of the same exquisite black silk.

Tears stung her eyes.

He shuffled close beside her, his brows furrowing. "I only wanted to give you something reminiscent of your mother's embroidery." She had lost the scrap of silk that held her mother's swan somewhere between the tavern and the Teranos Estate.

"I know it meant a lot to you. I didn't mean to upset you, love."

She shook her head, scrubbing at her eyes. "I am just . . ." She shook her head again and hugged the dress to her breast. "This means so much to me, Killian. I love it so much. I love you."

He beamed as he strode to sit by the edge of their bed. "Then I'll have a new one made until I fill your wardrobe with every imaginable shade," he declared. "You might even start a new fashion. You should have seen the seamstress's face when I told her I wanted more grenadis fashioned from brocades of dancing bears, pigs, and goats. She even laughed when I mentioned featherless owls."

An inelegant snort erupted from her nose and giggles bubbled from her throat. "You didn't!"

"I did." He pulled her onto his lap, cradling her against his chest. "With every new grenadi, I'll bring you to one new place in the realm . . . anywhere you wish to go, my elorin."

Tears trickled from her eyes. Mailin threw her arms around his neck but quickly jumped back before she crushed her new grenadi. She smoothed it out with a reverent caress. "Well, there is one place I'd like to go."

He arched a questioning brow.

"Madam Sima's."

His mouth parted. *"What?"*

"I'd like to invite Leisa to come to Amereen with us." With Mailin's current employment, and being mated to Amereen's very own lord commander, she now had means to free her sister from bondage. There was no longer reason for Leisa to fear the journey to Amereen. She explained as much. "Will you warp me to Madam Sima's on your next day off?"

"You know I would warp you anywhere, my elorin, but not in this instance."

The smile slipped from her face. "Leisa won't impose on us, Killian. If she agrees to come, I'll use my wages to pay for her rent in the capital." She had even worked out an employment opportunity for Leisa. Saoire had agreed to take on a waitress.

He chuckled. "That was not my concern, love. I am just not confident warping more than one person at a time." He tugged at the ends of her unbraided hair, still outlandishly short for a woman in court. "I'll go alone and bring her back if she agrees."

Tension ebbed from her spine. She curled her arms over his shoulders and pulled him in for a kiss to convey the depth of her appreciation. The man was truly a gift from the gods. Speaking of gifts . . . Mailin wiggled from his arms and snatched up her new outfit.

She skipped to the framed mirror by the dresser and held the silken garment against herself. Gorgeous.

Killian strode up behind her.

"Undo my laces," she commanded, rocking on the balls of her feet with unconcealed excitement. "I want to try it on."

Obediently, he proceeded to untie the ribbons at the back of her dress. She shimmied out of it, but instead of helping her into her new dress, he hung it over the chair.

"Later," he murmured.

Mailin made a noise of protest but quickly fell silent as he proceeded to remove his scabbard and baldric. His gauntlets came off next, followed by his lightweight cuirass. He stripped off his tunic and undid the buckle on his belt.

He tugged his belt free, his gaze locked on hers. The air in the room began to swelter, and her breaths came out in soft pants as she ogled him with shameless appreciation. Shirtless, scarred, and wrapped in sinful slabs of muscle. All hers.

She sashayed up to him and traced the glowing sunburst pattern that had been etched over his heart when they mated. Her fingers slid further down. "One, two, three . . ."

He stood patiently still as she counted all eight of his perfectly sculpted abs—something that had become a recent habit. He chuckled as she neared the vee of muscle that dipped into his pants, his knowing smirk so ridiculously sexy that her legs trembled in wanton anticipation.

He picked her up and settled them both on the bed. "I have another surprise for you."

"Do you?" she asked with a breathless laugh. "What is it?"

He rolled atop her, his hips sliding with familiar ease to settle at the juncture of her thighs. He gave her a nudge, hard and insistent. A sly smile curved his lips. "Would you like to have it?"

Mailin giggled. Her skin tingled as his lips brushed above her heart where her mating mark mirrored his.

"Oh, yes, *please*. I do love surprises."

THE END

ACKNOWLEDGMENTS

People say writing a book is hard. No one said anything about the acknowledgements. When I gleefully sat myself down to pen this section, I thought it would be easy. After all, I already did all the hard work with Mailin and Killian's story. And really, how hard can it be to say thank you?

Imagine my shock as I stared at the blinking cursor for a good hour before I came to the terrifying realisation that this section is arguably as hard as writing another chapter in the book. Gosh, where do I even start? Do I mention every name? What about the people who have indirectly influenced my writing? (The guy who invented coffee is high on this list).

So many hands have gone into helping me get to this point of publication that it would be a massive plot hole, so to speak, to miss a single person. After much consideration, here is my feeble attempt:

A shoutout to my ridiculously large and loving family. My son, my parents, my three beautiful sisters, my brothers-in-law, my horde of nieces and nephews, and my wonderful in-laws who love and put up with me simply because. There is nothing more special than knowing you are loved unconditionally, and it is that knowledge that has given me confidence in most everything I do in life, and the belief that I can write.

Denali Day, my critique partner–turned-confidant, without whom I probably (not joking) would still be obsessively writing and rewriting my first manuscript to this day. It is your constant and generous praise that spurred me to write that next book, and your friendship just keeps me sane. Somewhere along the way, you also became that tiny voice in my head whispering just do it—so I did. Thank you for being an inspiration; thank you for being my source of courage.

Kelley Luna, my bookish soulmate-turned-editor, without whom this book would no doubt be published as a pale imitation of its

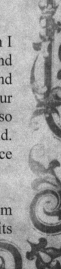

current form. I thank God daily for your (uncanny) grammatical prowess, infectious enthusiasm, and your unfailing support (even if you are a disruptive force to my TBR list). You have truly spoilt me in the best sense of the word. Thank you for tirelessly waving those proverbial pom-poms in my face; thank you for being my source of confidence.

Liv Arnold, who has been there for me when my writing was greener than grass. Thank you for sharing my journey as well as yours. It makes a world of difference knowing I can reach out any day, any time, and you're always there.

Courtney Kelly, whose attention to detail blows me away every time. Thank you for your enthusiasm with every story, your skill with plot inconsistencies, and constructive story suggestions.

Ivy Williams, you'll go down in history as the first reader to have brought tears to my eyes—for the best possible reason. Every author needs a reader like you.

Tina Emmerich, your eagle eyes are every author's boon. Your enthusiasm is a delicious bonus.

Kyra Halland, your kind words are greatly appreciated.

Lana Pechercyzk, Tanya Bird, and Davina Stone for just being awesome with a capital A. Thank you for entertaining my random queries and sharing invaluable advice to boot!

Special shoutout to the Aspiring group at Romance Writers Australia. Ladies, you are all legends. Never let anyone tell you otherwise. Your collective love for the written word inspires me daily.

And last but not least, dear reader, thank you for taking a chance on me. I hope you enjoyed Mailin and Killian's story as much as I enjoyed writing it.

ABOUT THE AUTHOR

Hollee Mands used to be that kid who sat at the back of the class, scribbling stories and doodling in dreary math workbooks. Much older and still unrepentant, she's now determined to bring her imaginations to life through the keyboard. When she isn't squirrelling away time to write, read, or sketch, she is a communications consultant and proud mom to a tiny dictator who has the speech patterns (and physical energy) to rival a steam train. She currently resides in fickle-weathered Melbourne and is a proud member of Romance Writers Australia.

www.holleemands.com

Printed in the USA
CPSIA information can be obtained
at www.ICGtesting.com
LVHW092343051023
759999LV00040B/1095/J